WORTH

A NOVEL

NEW YORK TIMES BESTSELLING AUTHOR

DEBORAH BLADON

Also by Deborah Bladon

Chapter 1

Maya

I notice him immediately. It's impossible not to. Julian Bishop is the man of the hour, after all. This celebration, complete with expensive champagne and stiff-backed wait staff, has drawn the crème de la crème of Manhattan's social elite. It's the place to be tonight, and with a lot of crafty manipulation and a fair bit of luck, I'm standing in the midst of it, wearing a killer little black dress and diamond earrings I borrowed from a broker who has sold more than her fair share of apartments with Park Avenue addresses.

"I got you another glass of champagne, Maya."

I turn toward my date for the evening, taking the tall crystal flute from his hand. I enjoy a small sip while I look at his hands. They're adequate, not too large, and not too small. Those hands, along with the brief kiss he gave me when he picked me up tonight promise a night of passion that would be forgettable at best. He's nothing to write home about or to write about at all, for that matter.

"Thanks, Charlie," I purr. "Where's your drink?"

He nudges the sexy-as-all-hell, black-rimmed eyeglasses up the bridge of his nose with his index finger. He has a nerd with a side of male model look. That's what made me stop at his desk two weeks ago to ask if I could borrow his stapler.

I don't staple. If I did, I'm sure I'd find one in my desk, hidden beneath the three dresses and two pairs of shoes I have tucked in the drawer. I never know when a change of wardrobe is called for. A girl has to be ready for anything when she's trying to claw her way up the hierarchy of the real estate market in this town.

"I had one. That's my limit." He squints as he looks at the bar. "Is she here yet? I heard someone say she's going to make an entrance."

I heard someone say she's a dirty, dirty slut.

That, someone, was me. I said it to myself. She's far from dirty or slutty. She's a lawyer, Harvard educated, with looks to rival her intelligence.

Jealousy is a filthy accessory, and I don't wear it well.

"I don't think she's arrived yet." I turn back to where Julian is standing. He looks just as he did when I first laid eyes on him. That was more than a year ago. I was helping a friend, and he was offering her a job. Our paths crossed, the energy flowed, and then he left.

I never saw the man in person again.

I would have settled for one tumble in the sheets of his bed. A brief encounter would have satisfied my craving, but it wasn't meant to be. He continued on his happily-ever-after path, and I sailed the dating waters of Manhattan occasionally snagging a Charlie in my net.

2

"I'm going to mingle," I say it like I mean it. "I'll meet you back here in thirty."

Charlie looks down at his watch. It's not impressive. That's not Charlie's style.

"Thirty minutes, Maya." He touches the lenses of his glasses with the tips of two of his fingers before he points them right at me. "I'm going to have my eyes on you."

Good for you, Cowboy.

I take my champagne, my spirit of adventure, and my too tight black heels and I start to cross the room. I took my time getting dressed tonight in anticipation of that split second we all live for. It's that moment when the man you imagine running naked through a field of daisies with or fucking in a back alley, turns to looks at you.

I've been planning this accidental meeting between Julian and me for weeks, including carefully plotting every word I'll say when his eyes meet mine.

I'm counting on him remembering me because I've been told that I'm not easy to forget.

"Maya Baker." The voice behind me is unmistakably his. It's warm with a hint of control and deep with the promise of pleasure.

I start to pivot at the sound of it. It's a beacon, a pull that is too strong to resist.

"Don't turn around." A hand, steady and determined, touches my hip. The fingers assert enough pressure to control my movement. "I don't recall seeing your name on the guest list." Something's caught Julian's cock's attention. I can feel the length of it pressing against me in the middle of the room while we wait for his business partner,

3

rumored lover and woman I'd most like to lock in a closet for eternity to arrive. "I was a last minute addition."

"A welcome addition," he adds. "Are you enjoying yourself?"

I feel the undercurrent of desire. It was there over a year ago when we met. It's stronger now.

"I am now." I push my fingers into his on my hip.

His chest lifts and then falls on a heavy exhale. "I'm needed at the podium. You won't run away before we have a chance to talk, will you?"

I turn to look up at him. Black hair, ocean blue eyes and a face that could make a woman want to lock her office door mid-day to fantasize about him.

I've done it more than once.

"You're as handsome as ever, Julian." I lower my voice. "I'm available to talk whenever you are."

He rounds me, his hand still holding mine. "You're more enchanting than the day we met, Maya. I've followed your career. I have a position I think you'd be interested in."

"What position might that be, Julian?" A woman's voice asks from behind me.

I don't have to turn to know who asked the question. I've heard her speak enough times this past year that I would recognize her throaty tone anywhere.

Isadora Patel, Julian's girlfriend, is not only a highly regarded attorney; she's also an advocate for women's issues in the workplace. She's been the keynote speaker at two conferences I attended. Both of those were focused on women in business.

For someone I want to hate, I admit I have a lot of respect for her.

"We'll discuss it later." Julian's hand drops mine. "I'm about to take the stage, Isadora."

"We're about to take the stage," she corrects him. "Introduce me to your friend."

I know that I shouldn't get in the middle of whatever is happening between them right now, but since I'm physically in the middle, I turn to face her.

She's a stunning woman and that's as true tonight as it's been every time I've seen her. Isadora's taller than me by at least six inches. Her long blonde hair is pulled back into a high ponytail and her brown eyes are framed by long lashes.

The strapless black dress she's wearing may bear the same designer label as the one I have on, but it's tailored to fit her every curve. It's obvious that she didn't pick it up off the rack.

"I'm Maya Baker." I extend a hand toward her, surprised that I'm not trembling. "I've heard only great things about you, Ms. Patel."

"Maya," she repeats back my name as her gaze volleys from my face to Julian's. "You were at the leadership in business summit two months ago. I remember you."

I hear the instant relief in her tone as she reaches for my hand. She gives it a firm shake before she pulls back. I'm no longer a threat in her eyes. She thinks I'm an admirer.

"Your speech was enlightening." In my experience, genuine compliments are the most effective tension breaker, at least when it comes to other women. "I'm glad I had the chance to hear it."

"It was an important topic." She studies my face. Her eyes trail over my shoulder length black hair, blue eyes, and pale pink lips. "I'm surprised to see you here tonight."

She's surprised that her boyfriend was holding my hand when she approached us. I no longer have to wonder why Julian asked me not to turn around. His plus one was keeping an eye on her man from across the room.

"My date had an invite for two, so I tagged along." If I were going to be completely truthful, I'd confess that the only reason I'm here tonight is so I can talk to Julian.

She smiles at me. "I hope you and your date are both enjoying yourselves."

I can't speak for Charlie, but I was having the time of my life until she showed up. It's time to make myself scarce. "I should get back to him."

Isadora reaches out to stop me with a hand on my forearm. "I'm curious how you know Julian. You two seem like old friends."

Apparently, jealousy isn't in short supply tonight. The green-eyed monster has its claws in Isadora too.

"Maya and I met some time ago at Falon Shaw's studio," Julian answers from behind me.

"Ah." Isadora squeezes my arm. "So you're a photographer too? Julian has been anxious to find someone to shoot the interiors of our new residential suites. If you send a few sample shots to the manager of our marketing department, she'll let you know if we're interested."

My close friend, Falon Shaw, should have that job. She's done work for Bishop Hotels in the past. As much as I'm tempted to point that out, I let it slide. Falon can do her own bidding. She doesn't need me to pitch her name. She's an established photographer whose work speaks volumes.

"Maya?" Charlie moves into view behind Isadora just as I'm about to tell her that I'm in real estate, not photography. "I have another glass of champagne for you."

Since I'm still holding onto an almost full glass of bubbly, I shoot Charlie a look, but he's eyeing Isadora's ass like it's a treasure he's been searching a lifetime for. "I'm good. I was about to come find you, Charlie."

Charlie takes that as his cue. He steps forward, introduces himself to Isadora and launches into a discussion that's peppered with legal terms I don't understand.

I take the opportunity to turn back to Julian.

His eyes meet mine instantly. "I still have your business card, Maya. Is the contact information on it current? Can I reach you at that number?"

My phone number is one of the few things in my life that hasn't changed since I first met him. I've transitioned from being a rental agent to an associate broker. I moved to a new neighborhood and I've dated some of the most interesting men in this city and a couple of duds too.

When I handed him that card in Falon's studio, I wasn't sure what I hoped would come from it. We had a very brief conversation before he offered her a job photographing the interior of The Bishop Hotel in

Tribeca. He told me that he'd consider me if he were ever looking for a rental, but I never heard from him again. I assumed my card was tossed in the trash and I became a non-existent memory.

"You can reach me at the number on the card," I say politely knowing full well that even though I can hear Isadora engaging in small talk with Charlie, her gaze is glued to her boyfriend and me.

"I'll be in touch, Maya."

I blink at him as he moves around me to talk to Charlie and Isadora. I don't bother trying to hear what he's saying to them.

I came to this event to arrange a face-to-face meeting with him.

This party is a celebration of his newest hotel, which contains a dozen luxury residential suites. I'm determined to secure a shot at selling those. When Julian reaches out to me, I'm going to convince the man that I'm exactly what he needs.

I'd jump at the chance to prove that I'm what he needs in bed, but his sheets are already being warmed by someone else.

He's committed to Isadora and I'm committed to my career.

I want in on his business, and I'll do whatever it takes to show him that I'm the woman for the job.

Chapter 2

Julian

When I agreed to the launch party for our new hotel in Chelsea, I assumed it would be as dull as every other event Bishop Hotels has hosted for the past few years.

The routine is the same regardless of the location. I mingle, Isadora shows up late, and we take the stage together to make a surprise announcement about a secret project that our marketing department strategically leaked to travel industry bloggers and reporters weeks ago.

Last night was different.

It wasn't because my younger sister accepted the marriage proposal of her boyfriend during the party. Brynn delivered that news to me in person near the end of the night just as she was ready to leave with her now-fiancé, Smith Booth. I'm happy for them. Marriage is what they both want.

I was preoccupied during much of the event with the sight of Maya with her date. He held her hand as she balanced against him when she adjusted the strap on one of her shoes. He smiled down at her when she laughed.

She was a welcome surprise during an otherwise uneventful evening.

"What happened to you last night?" Isadora looks up from where she's sitting behind her desk. "You left the party early."

I left as soon as Maya did. I saw no reason to stay to chat up the guests we'd strategically invited because of the size of their bank accounts.

The hotel we launched last night is a new venture for us. In addition to an unforgettable experience for guests who choose to stay the night with us, we're offering a unique opportunity for a select few individuals.

The property has a dozen residential units. Each offers a stunning view of the city and comes with every amenity the hotel has to offer. It's a risky gamble in the current volatile market, but it's going to pay off.

With the right broker on board, the residential suites will sell themselves.

"I left as it was winding down." I step into her office to drop a contract on her desk. "Have someone look this over by the end of the day. It's urgent."

She fingers the corner of the papers. "I'll handle it myself."

Isadora was hired on as a junior attorney over three years ago. Now, she runs the legal department at Bishop Hotels.

Our professional lives are tangled around her employment contract and the shares I gifted her with a year-and-a-half ago when she first hinted that she wanted an engagement ring.

A diamond on her finger is still the thing she craves most in the world. I can't bring myself to walk within ten feet of a jewelry store.

I may have felt close to her at one time, but that's not the case anymore. She's someone I've come to rely heavily on for business advice.

It's a primarily professional relationship that is occasionally punctuated with an unfulfilling fuck.

"What do you want to do for dinner tonight?" She pushes back from her desk to stand. She's wearing a white blouse and a gray pencil skirt. Isadora is every inch the professional when she's in this building.

"I'm having dinner with Sebastian." I hold her gaze waiting for the question I know will follow.

"Why didn't you invite me to join you?" She walks toward me. "Zeb would love to see me."

He wouldn't. Sebastian Wolf spends his days and often, his nights, as a valued member of the NYPD's homicide squad. He's clashed with Isadora on more than one occasion. She may not be an expert in criminal law, but she was vocal about some of the media reports of a high profile case that Sebastian was an integral part of.

She has no idea he was one of the detectives assigned to a murder case that eventually resulted in the acquittal of the suspect who just happened to be a senator's son. Isadora worked on the senator's re-election campaign last term. Her loyalty lies with him, not with the truth.

"You'll find something to keep yourself busy." My gaze drops to the patterned area rug that covers the hardwood floor.

Her fingertips trail over the fabric that covers my bicep. "Maybe I'll go shopping for a wedding gift for your sister and her fiancé."

I study her face. It's flawless, as usual. Her make-up is applied with the same precision as her attention to every word on each contract that crosses her desk. "You heard about their engagement."

The news should have come from me, but I knew where that discussion would take us.

"They've barely been together for six months and she's wearing a ring." She reaches for my shoulder. "We've been dating for three years and my finger is still bare."

Dating.

That's how I've always defined what this is. We don't live together. We rarely sleep together. I wear a condom each time we do fuck to avoid the possibility that a child will bind us forever. There are many things I trust Isadora with but not getting pregnant isn't one of them.

I don't want her to have my baby, so I take equal responsibility for making certain that doesn't happen.

"I have no interest in getting married." I step back so I'm out of her reach. "Nothing has changed since the last time we had this discussion."

She matches my step with one of her own, closing the distance between us in an instant. She stands on her tiptoes to brush her lips over my cheek. "You're wrong about that, darling. Something has changed. I'm getting older."

"You won't be thirty for another three months." I wave my hand at the calendar hanging on her office wall. "I just hit that milestone, and I don't consider myself ancient yet."

"You don't have eggs that are on a timer." She pats her stomach. "This is the ideal time for us to start a family. I want us to be married before that happens."

We circle the same subject every few months. I've always made it clear to her that I don't envision the same future between us as she does. "Isadora, when I say I'm not interested in getting married, I'm serious."

She sighs. "You're not serious about that, Julian. We've been together for more than three years. If we're not headed toward marriage, where exactly is this going?"

It's a direct question she's never asked me before. I've stayed with her because it's been convenient and easy, but our relationship has been stagnant for a long time. Our connection has been heavily focused on the business for years now. The drive to grow the hotel chain has kept us bound to each other. It's all we talk about when we're together.

I stare at her face, realizing that I'll never give her what she needs and she'll never be what I want. "I am serious. I'm not going to marry you, not now, not ever."

"Do you love me?" She shoots the question out so quickly that I take a step back physically. Her bottom lip quivers. She's not easily overcome with emotion. I've never seen her shed a tear.

"Isadora," I say her name before I exhale on an exasperated breath. "The office isn't the place to discuss this."

"That's not an answer."

"I care about what happens to you." I hold her gaze.

"You don't love me?" She doesn't try to mask the surprise in her voice. "You seriously don't love me?"

I've never said those three words to her even though she's whispered them in my ear when we've been in bed together. I couldn't bring myself to say them, knowing that they weren't weighted with the truth.

"Answer me." Her tone shifts from calm to obvious irritation. "Just say it, Julian. Tell me you don't love me and that I'm wasting my time loving you."

Unexpected relief washes over me. I know the fucked up mess that the next words out of my mouth are going to cause. I've put everything I have into this business and when I end this, I'll lose a piece of it to the woman standing in front of me.

That was a sacrifice I was never willing to make, so I kept things between us as is but now, the price is miniscule compared to the scent of freedom in the air.

"I don't love you." I look directly into her eyes as I say the words so there's no misinterpretation.

A pained sound escapes from between her lips. Her eyes search mine for something more; a hint that I'm hiding my true feelings even though I just spoke them, loudly and clearly. All she sees is my resolution to finally end our relationship.

She glances back at her desk and the thick stack of papers I dropped there. "I'll have the contract back to you by mid-afternoon. I'll send someone by your apartment to pick up my things before the end of the week."

I make my way out of her office and down the hall to my own without another word. The relief I feel almost brings me to my knees. I'm no longer drowning in a pool of infinite need. It's over. It was time. Isadora knows it in her heart. Now she needs to let go of what could have been so she can face the reality of what is. I just hope to hell my company can survive.

Chapter 3

Maya

"I heard you made it to the Bishop event last night." Anne, the owner of the real estate brokerage firm I work for, nudges my elbow. "Your balls are bigger than most of the men who work here."

I take it as a compliment. I've hauled ass since day one. Anne was the one who hired me on as a rental agent a few years ago. She took me under her wing. The woman has gone to bat for me more than once. The least I can do is finagle my way into a party to try and get a shot at the contract for the residential suites inside the newest Bishop property.

"Charlie needed a plus one." I flash a smile as I fill my coffee mug. "He had an invite."

"Charlie in legal?" She glances at the long corridor to our left. "I didn't realize you two knew each other."

We didn't until the day I stopped by his desk to ask to borrow his stapler. When he asked me out on the spot, I said yes because he was cute. We went to dinner, then a movie and after the ending credits rolled, we said goodnight in front of the theatre when he gave me a chaste kiss on my cheek.

Two days later when I was waiting for a new client in the reception area, a courier dropped off a pristine white envelope with Charlie's name written across it in raised lettering. The receptionist called

Charlie to tell him that there was a delivery from Bishop Hotels at the front desk.

I knew immediately what was in the envelope. Every person in real estate in the five boroughs wanted an invite to the Bishop party. I held out hope that I'd make it onto the guest list, but I didn't. For some reason, that I still don't understand, Charlie did.

I struck up a conversation about the movie we'd seen as he opened the envelope and when he read the invitation and then looked at me with a question in his eyes, I answered. I told him I'd love to go with him. He broke out a huge grin and the receptionist waited for us to kiss.

That didn't happen.

"We're acquaintances," I qualify. "We went to the party, and then he dropped me off at home. That's where the office gossip ends."

She laughs even though she's notorious for spreading rumors. There's never any ill intent behind it. Anne craves drama. Everyone who works at Carvel Properties International knows to be on high alert if they see Anne near the coffee machine whispering in someone's ear.

So far, I haven't gotten caught up in any of the office scandals.

"What did you find out about the residential suites in their newest hotel?" She leans closer and drops her tone to a hushed whisper. "Have they picked a listing agent yet?"

I shake my head. I used the age-old tactic of standing near the entrance to the corridor that leads to the washrooms before Charlie and I left. I know, from experience, that many high powered conversations begin in those awkward spaces and that's exactly what happened last night.

Two of the male Bishop board members came out of the washroom at the same time. As they breezed past where I was standing on their way back to the party, I overheard them talking about the fact that Julian hadn't chosen a broker for the project yet.

"We still have a chance?" Anne grabs my shoulder and gives me a good shake. "Do you know what this means?"

I look at where her hand is pressed against the navy blue fabric of my dress. I know exactly what it means, but I know that whenever the firm takes on a large project, Anne assigns one of the senior sales agents or associate brokers to take the reins.

"I'm going to send Dax over to Julian Bishop's office after lunch." She claps her hands together. "If anyone from Carvel can land that account, it'll be him."

It won't be him. It'll be me. "Last night Julian mentioned that he planned on calling me."

"For what reason?" She eyes the donuts on the table next to us but doesn't move to pick one up.

"I'm hoping he'll call to offer me the listing," I answer.

Anne glances at me. "Your biggest sale was your best friend's apartment, Maya."

I know that. When Falon and her husband decided to move, they hired me to sell their place. I did a stellar job, and the commission check was the largest I've ever received.

Obviously, I got that job because of my connection to her. It was a boost to my career since there's a prominent quote from Falon's husband, Asher Foster, on my profile page on the Carvel website. Asher's a rock star. He's a literal, award-winning singer.

His endorsement resulted in three other musicians seeking me out so I could sell their places. Not one of those properties listed above the million dollar mark, but I sold each apartment quickly and in all three cases, I was able to negotiate a price that was close to list.

"I'm as qualified as anyone else in the office to sell those units," I say tightly.

Anne's gaze drops to the screen of her smartphone. "I'll hold off on sending Dax over to Bishop Headquarters until you hear from Julian. I want a word-for-word of what he says to you."

She'll get what she wants minus the harmless flirting that I already know will take place during the call. "You got it."

"Maya, I want you to know that I think you're as qualified as any of the senior sales staff." She picks up her coffee mug. "If you're given a shot at this, I'll back you up. You'll have full access to all my contacts, and I'll be at your beck and call twenty-four, seven."

That's why I love working with her. She'll do whatever she can to make certain I shine brighter than she does. "You're the best, Anne."

"You know it." She gestures toward my mug with a sly grin on her face. "Drink that coffee and get back to your desk. You need a solid sales approach in hand when you talk to Julian."

"I'm already on it." I tap my forehead. "I've got a million ideas in here that will translate to quick sales of those units."

That earns me a full-on smile and a wink.

I want the Bishop job because of what it will do for my career, but I'm also eager to land it for another reason. I know that Anne wants the firm's name front and center on the project. It will benefit us both. That's why I'm going to put my all into pursuing it.

Chapter 4

Julian

"There was a surprise guest at the party last night," I say before I draw a pull from the bottle of beer I ordered when I arrived. I beat Sebastian to this pub by a solid twenty minutes, and I was running late. His work is unpredictable. His devotion to it isn't.

We were friends long before he did his time at the police academy. I offered him a job as the head of security for the hotels, but his sights have always been set on being a detective. He's living his dream now, even if it's taking its toll on every other aspect of his life.

"Obviously it wasn't me," he jokes.

I didn't offer up an invitation to him this time around. He would have turned me down. He always does. Sebastian's never worn a tuxedo. I doubt he ever will. The dark blue suit he's wearing tonight is one of only a few he owns.

"Was it a welcome surprise?" he asks as he stares at my face. "A man or a woman?"

"A woman."

His brows shoot up. "Tell me Maya crashed your party."

"She was there," I confirm with a nod.

Sebastian blinks. "Did you man up and talk to her this time?"

I look across the bar to where two women are glancing in our direction. It's not uncommon for

Sebastian and me to be approached when we're out together. Neither of us has a wedding ring on.

"We spoke," I admit with a grin. "I can't tell you what it is about that woman, but my body reacted when I got within two feet of her."

He throws his head back and laughs. "Are we talking a Ms. Gordon worthy reaction or better than that?"

"Fuck you," I toss back with a chuckle.

Ms. Gordon was our eleventh-grade Algebra teacher. She was mid-twenties, beautiful and engaged to the principal of our high school. I didn't give a shit. My cock didn't either. I was hard through every second of every class I had with the woman.

Sebastian sat next to me. I gave up trying to hide the obvious erection in my jeans halfway through first semester.

"Was she alone?" He looks over at the two women I spotted earlier. Sebastian can take one, or both home if he chooses to, but he won't. He would have at one point, but he grew up around the time he was promoted to detective.

If he's interested in a woman, he'll ask her out to dinner. He'll get to know her intellectually before he beds her.

I glance at his profile. His face has obviously changed remarkably since we were kids, but the color of his hair and his eyes still closely resemble my own. He used to call me his brother, even though he already has two.

We're as close as blood relatives. He's one of the few people in this world I'll confide in. That's the only reason I told him about Maya a few months ago after I saw her having dinner with another man. She didn't notice me, but I couldn't take my eyes off of her.

My reaction to her was visceral and unexpected. I felt an overwhelming need to talk about it the next day. There are only two people on this earth who will never judge me and will hold a secret to the grave. One is Sebastian. The other is our mutual friend Griffin Kent. Both know about my illogical attraction to Maya Baker.

"She was on a date." I take another sip of the beer. "A guy named Charlie."

"Charlie?" He repeats the name back. "Did you meet Charlie?"

I wait for a beat. "Charlie couldn't tear his eyes away from Isadora."

"That, my friend, is irony at its best." He skims his fingertip over the rim of the glass of soda water in front of him. "Charlie wants Izzy. You want Maya. It sounds like the four of you should be playing a game of musical beds."

"Isadora and I are done." I drop my gaze to the top of the wooden bar. "Brynn got engaged last night, and Isadora pushed for the same this morning."

"You two broke up? You're shitting me."

"I'm not." I look at him. "It's over."

A wide smile takes over his mouth. "It's about fucking time, Julian. Jesus, I thought this day would never come."

I shoot him a wry glance. He's told me on more than one occasion that I was wasting my time with Isadora. He saw us together and the non-existent spark between us. I finally told him to shut the hell up about it months ago. It wasn't because I thought he was wrong, but the constant reminder that I needed to stop putting the business before everything else was the last thing I wanted to hear.

"How did she take it?"

I shrug. "The same way she takes everything. She was stoic, unreadable."

"You're expecting a fight, aren't you? Do you think she'll fight to hold onto you?"

I take a deep swallow of the beer before answering. "She can fight all she wants. I'm done. It's over."

"Good." He shoots me a smile. "You're free to chase after Maya now. Come to think of it, why the fuck are you here with me? Shouldn't you be buying her a drink tonight instead of watching me nurse a glass of water?"

"Did you miss the part where I said she came to the party with another man? I have no idea how serious that is." I wave a hand as I stand. "We're about to be propositioned, so unless you're interested in the women walking this way, I suggest we head next door for dinner."

He slides off the bar stool as he steals a glance at the approaching brunettes. "Italian food on your dime beats either of them. Think about what I said, Julian. You don't want to wake up one day ten years from now and look up Maya online to see that she's Mrs. Charlie Whatever-The-Fuck-His-Surname-Is."

Warton. I knew that before I spotted him with Maya last night.

I scanned the guest list after the invitations were sent out. Charles Warton Jr. has been on my radar for some time. Now, that he's a part of Maya's life, my interest piqued to a new level.

"I'll take your advice into consideration."

"You're such a stuck up prick sometimes." He pats my chest before he brushes past me. "I'm starving. Let's eat."

Chapter 5

Maya

"I have a new listing appointment in an hour."
I tap my fingertip against the face of the antique silver
wristwatch I'm wearing.

It doesn't work. Most of the vintage watches
I've picked up over the years can't keep time. I don't
buy them to help keep me punctual. I'm always on
time. My phone keeps me on track with its calendar
app and the multitude of alarms that all signal
different, but equally important, events.

The wind chime I just heard is a reminder of a
meeting I have with a potential client on the Upper
West Side.

"Your watch is running two hours slow,
Maya." Charlie cranes his neck so he can get a better
view of my wrist. "You know that it's two o'clock and
not noon, right?"

"I know," I say impatiently. "I'm wearing it
because I like the style. That's the only reason I ever
wear a watch."

"I like you, Maya. You're different."

I smile in a way that says thank you. I know
he meant it as a compliment. If he were more my
type, I'd be inclined to accept the third date invitation
that he's about to offer me.

I've been involved with enough men to know
when one is interested. Charlie has strolled past my
office door every day since we went to the Bishop

party. I kept expecting him to stop to make small talk, but he hasn't until today.

"Do you want to have dinner with me tomorrow night?" he asks as he drags his hand through his brown hair.

I hate lying. It's useless to do it at work because when I have, I inevitably trip over my own words. I'm always caught in the untruth and whoever I was trying to deceive will either be hurt or pissed off at me, and neither of those scenarios works well in a business setting.

"I should clarify that it wouldn't be dinner with just me," Charlie says quietly, his light green eyes pinned to my face. "My dad and his wife invited us to dinner at the Axel location in Tribeca."

"Your parents want us to have dinner with them?"

My mind races as I wait for him to confirm what he just said to me. He wants me to meet his parents? We've gone out twice. We haven't even kissed. In my world, that means I'm not ready to meet his doorman yet, let alone his parents.

"He called me twenty minutes ago to invite us. I told him about you last week. I didn't have a chance to explain that we're not officially a couple." He shrugs that off as his gaze drops. "It's just that he's thinking of selling his apartment and I know you'd be the right broker for the job."

"Your parents are moving?"

He visibly cringes at my question. "My mom lives in Arizona. My dad lives here with his third wife."

I nod, not wanting to waste time by delving into the finer points of the uncomfortable dynamics of the Warton clan, I ask the obvious question. "Where does your dad live?"

"Central Park West."

My chest tightens as my heart pumps faster. The listing price of any property located on that street comes with so many zeroes that I feel like my head is about to spin around from pure excitement.

I don't want to string Charlie along, but it's just a dinner. There's no reason why we can't share a nice meal and good conversation with his dad and his stepmom. On the way home from the restaurant I'll let him down gently by telling him that I'd make a better friend than a girlfriend for him.

They're not just empty words. I do think that Charlie and I would make great friends.

"I think we should go to that dinner."

His head whips up in surprise. "You'll go with me?"

I nod. "I'd love to meet your dad and his wife."

He fingers the edge of the frame of his eyeglasses as he contemplates my response. "I'll call him back and tell him we'll be there."

I glance down at my phone's screen. "I need to get to my listing appointment."

"I'll find you tomorrow so we can coordinate the pick-up plan."

"The pick-up plan?"

"The plan for when I pick you up at your place for our date," he says that with a grin. "Dinner's at eight. If you want I can come by at six for a pre-dinner drink."

"I have a showing at five tomorrow afternoon, but I'll be ready to go by seven-thirty."

I don't see an ounce of disappointment in his expression. "Good luck with the listing appointment. You don't need luck to get the job though. Who could resist you?"

My lip twitches into an almost smile. "You sure know how to boost a girl's ego, Charlie. I'll see you tomorrow night."

"If not before, Maya." He bows and waves his arm in the air.

He's everything I should want in a guy, but the only man I can think about is the one who holds the keys to the twelve residential suites in the new Bishop hotel in his hands.

It's been days since Julian said he'd be in touch. I've left two messages with his assistant and still, I've heard nothing back.

As I head out the office door, I make a note in my phone's calendar to stop by the Bishop corporate offices the day after tomorrow if my calls still aren't returned. A little initiative is never a bad thing in this industry. Besides, I'll take any chance I can get to see Julian in person.

***

"I happen to think Charlie is a catch." My younger sister, Matilda, pours a splash of cream into her coffee cup before she snaps the plastic lid back on. "He's cute, he's got a great job, and he treats you right. What more could you ask for, Maya?"

Sparks? A pounding heartbeat when I look at him? Wet panties when he looks at me?

"He's a nice guy, Tilly," I acquiesce as I take a sip of the herbal tea I ordered. I reached my self-imposed limit of three cups of coffee before noon today. If I hope to get any sleep tonight, I have to stick to non-caffeinated beverages for the rest of the evening. "He's just not my type."

Her blue eyes widen as she smiles. "You say that every time a guy is interested in you. There are only so many types of men walking the face of this earth. Sooner or later, you'll have to decide which type is right for you."

"So maybe I don't have a type." I wrinkle my nose. "I want a man who is different than anyone I've ever met before."

"You and me both." She taps her cup to mine. "I have another blind date tomorrow night."

This is the third one this month. I give Tilly credit for actively chasing after the happily-ever-after she wants. As adventurous as she is when it comes to dating, she's just as cautious.

"I can't be your bodyguard tomorrow night." I look over my shoulder at the entrance to the café. I'm meeting a client here in ten minutes to present an offer on her apartment. It may be seven p.m. but my day isn't over yet.

"The meeting the parents thing with Charlie is tomorrow?" Her dark brows lift. I can tell she's surprised. The first words out of her mouth when I met her here was a question about how my date with

Charlie had gone. Since she helped me get ready for the Bishop Hotel party, she deserved to know every boring detail. I didn't stop there. I also clued her in about Charlie's invitation to have dinner with his folks. "Promise me you'll at least keep an open mind. Third dates are almost always better than first and second dates. You know what they say about the third time being a charm."

I'm not about to tell her that the man I'm most excited to see tomorrow night isn't the one picking me up. It's his father. Tilly is a veterinary assistant. She's devoted her life to caring for animals and managing the feelings of the people who own them. She doesn't understand how ruthless a person has to be in real estate.

"I agreed to have dinner with him, didn't I?" I smile. "You'll be alright on your date, won't you? I'm sorry I can't be there spying on you while I drink a martini and you sit a few feet away pretending you don't know me."

She laughs. "You know how much I appreciate you watching over me when I meet strange men. Knowing you're close makes me feel safe."

"Where are you meeting this mystery man?"

She looks around the crowded café. "I think I'll ask him to meet me here. I doubt like hell he'd try anything while I'm holding a hot cup of coffee."

"Good plan." I look back when I hear the door open. I wave to my client as soon as she makes eye contact with me. "It's time for me to work. Text me after your date tomorrow, or don't if you decide to take him home with you."

She pushes her long brown hair back over her shoulder. "I'll text you when I'm home. Good luck with Charlie. Remember what I said about third dates, Maya. Your life might change tomorrow night."

I'm counting on it. If all goes well, by this time next week, I'll be selling an apartment on Central Park West.

Chapter 6

Julian

As I walk into the restaurant, I take one look around and feel a surge of satisfaction at the full dining room.

I don't manage this aspect of the business. I have a team for that. We were approached early on by a restaurateur named Hunter Reynolds who wanted to establish a Tribeca location of his popular eatery. That's how Axel Tribeca was conceived. It launched when the attached hotel opened early last year. Both have surpassed my expectations.

I benefit from the steady stream of diners in the form of a percentage of the restaurant's profits. Hunter benefits in the same respect along with the glowing reviews. It's been a win-win for us both, and we've already discussed the possibility of teaming up for our new location in Philadelphia that will launch two years from now.

"Mr. Bishop?" A young blond woman wearing the required attire of a simple black dress approaches me. "Ms. Newell said I should be expecting you. She's waiting at the table you requested."

When you're faced with the prospect of going to battle against the best attorney you know, you hire the second best to represent you. That's the reason why I'm meeting Chloe Newell, an expert in employment law for dinner.

I stop a server as he passes by me. "I'd like a scotch neat brought to my table immediately."

He doesn't hesitate as he heads toward the bar to my left.

"Is Hunter here tonight?" I turn back to the hostess.

Her eyes dart to my face. "He was in earlier but left. I can call him back if you'd like."

The man has two children and a wife who spends too much time at the hospital where she works as a doctor. If he's left this to go to them, I'm not about to interrupt. "No, that's fine."

"Shall I show you to your table now?"

I've put off the inevitable for too long. I was hopeful that Isadora and I could work out an agreement ourselves that would sever our ties, but that's not going to happen. Every attempt I've made to speak to her the past few days has been met with silence.

Bringing Chloe on board is a strictly strategic move. I know Isadora well enough to realize that at some point she's going to strike and I need to be prepared.

"Lead the way," I say after glancing once more around the room.

"You'll be pleased to know that our special tonight is pan-fried duck breast," she says over her shoulder as she weaves her way around guests waiting to be seated, servers and the chef who popped out of the kitchen to make small talk with a couple who appear to be celebrating a birthday based on the cake on their table. "It's served with a red wine and orange sauce. I sampled it earlier, sir, and I'd recommend it highly. I don't think I've ever tasted anything better than that. It's perfection."

Perfection.

I won't find it on a plate or in the glass of scotch I ordered that is already being delivered to the table where Chloe is seated waiting for me.

Perfection is the woman sitting across the dining room.

Maya Baker's eyes catch mine as I approach my table. A small smile tugs at the corner of her full lips before she turns her attention back to the man seated next to her. Charles Warton, Sr., his current wife and his son, Charlie, are all engrossed in whatever Maya is saying.

It looks like I underestimated Charlie's importance to Maya. I wasn't expecting to stumble on a Warton family dinner, but now that I have, it's going to be near impossible to focus on anything but how incredible Maya looks tonight.

***

I scratch my chin while I listen to Chloe outline the approach she wants to take. She's on top of her game. I've used her services in the past when Isadora was out with the flu and I needed someone to negotiate with a senior executive I fired without warning.

Chloe took over and within three days, the man had a severance package that put a smile on his face, and I was just as satisfied since I only had to part with a fraction of what he might have been entitled to if Chloe wouldn't have found a small loophole that Isadora had written into his contract.

"I can start on this tomorrow morning, if you give me the go-ahead, Julian."

I tear my gaze away from Maya to look at her. She's garnered a few glances from some of the men dining at the tables near us. It's not surprising. Chloe's a beautiful woman. Blond hair, hazel eyes, and a sweet smile are all punctuated by a soft voice.

She's disarming which makes her perfect to take over when Isadora leaves her post.

"Come work for me, Chloe."

"No." She laughs. "I told you on the phone earlier that I'm not interested, Julian. I work for myself. Why the hell would I give that up to work for you?"

The woman has a point.

"I will take on this job because I love a good challenge." She sighs. "Once we get Isadora to sign off on her severance package, I'll put out some feelers and see who is looking. Does that work?"

I glance over her shoulder at Maya's table just in time to see Charlie kiss her cheek.

"That works." I wave at the server who has been patiently checking on us every few minutes since I sat down. "Are you ready to order?"

"Since you're paying me by the hour, I should stall, but I'm starving." She sighs. "I'm going to go with the duck and red wine sauce. It's the special tonight. What do you want?"

The only thing I want in this restaurant is Maya Baker and judging by the way she keeps looking in my direction, the feeling is mutual.

Chapter 7

Maya

I know it's impolite to stare but whoever coined that phrase has never seen Julian Bishop in a light gray two-piece suit with a black dress shirt underneath. He's not wearing a tie, which means a sliver of the skin on the top of his chest is visible.

I'm going to add that to the mental images I have of him, so when I go home tonight, I'll have fresh material for my fantasies.

"Maya?" Charlie's voice breaks through my thoughts. "My dad was asking if you grew up in New York."

I turn to look at Charles. He's a more distinguished version of Charlie with salt and pepper hair. If I was into men old enough to be my dad, I might have reacted more favorably when he tried to play footsie with me under the table. Instead, I scooted closer to Charlie, which sent the wrong message to him.

I'm essentially trapped in the middle of a Warton man sandwich and I haven't even ordered my entrée yet.

The only thing that isn't making this night a complete disaster is the fact that Julian is sitting in my direct line of sight. I just wish that I knew who the blonde across the table from his is. It's definitely not Isadora.

"I grew up in San Francisco."

"I've always wanted to go there," Hazel, Charlie's current stepmother, pipes up. The woman has barely said two words since we sat down to join her and her husband for dinner.

I admit that I had no idea what to expect when Charlie told me that Hazel was his father's third wife. I assumed she'd be closer to my age. I know more than a few twenty-five-year-old women married to men who are decades older than they are.

When I worked primarily in handling rentals, many of my clients were middle-aged men on the market for a rental for their much younger lover. A good percentage of those relationships turned into second or third marriages and vacancies when the man would invest in an apartment with a view for his new wife while trying to navigate a messy divorce.

My rental agent career taught me more about the dynamics of marriage within the ranks of Manhattan's elite than it did real estate.

"I think you'd like it." I look at Hazel. Her blue eyes are rimmed by the signs of age. Kindness lives in her smile. She reminds me of my mom, which makes me feel even more out of place.

"We should go." Charles pats her hand. "Our third honeymoon. You'd like that sweetie, wouldn't you?"

That brings more brightness to Hazel's face than the first glass of wine she had did. "Maya, you'll help me plan the trip, won't you?"

If it means I can sell their apartment for them, I'll take them on a personal tour of the City by the Bay and I'll even carry their luggage.

"First things first." Charles reaches to cover my hand with his. "Let's talk about young love."

Let's not.

"They're so adorable," Hazel says quietly as the server approaches. "I'm ordering a bottle of champagne so we can toast to love."

"To love?" I ask tightly.

"Look at you two." She nods her chin toward Charlie and me. "You two remind me of…"

"We work together," I interrupt.

She turns her full attention to me. "Maybe you don't feel it yet, Maya, but it's plain as day. You and Charlie are more than co-workers. I know love when it's right in front of me."

Charlie reaches his hand to fish for mine under the table. I pull back and toss him a warning glance. I'm not about to offer him any false hope born from the skewed view of what these people think they see.

"Maya's different than anyone I've ever met, "Charlie says as he looks into my eyes. "Our relationship is new, but I'm hopeful. Maybe one day we'll be as much in love as the two of you."

I almost roll my eyes at that. The entire taxi ride here, Charlie complained under his breath about having to see Hazel. One cocktail later and she's apparently his new favorite stepmom.

"Maybe after Maya sells our apartment, the four of us can fly out to San Francisco to meet her folks, son."

I ignore the comment Charles just made about meeting my parents as I turn in my chair to face him.

"Does this mean you're going to list the apartment with me?"

"Of course I am. Was there ever any doubt?" Charles arches a brow as he tosses me a playful wink.

Within the span of ten minutes I've landed the listing for his apartment, he's jumped to the conclusion that I'm crazy about his son and he can't stop flirting with me. This seems like the perfect time for me to excuse myself so I can freshen up in the ladies' room. I have a feeling it's going to be a long night.

Chapter 8

Julian

"Tell me if I'm wrong, but from where I was sitting, Charlie is far more interested in you than you are in him, Maya."

My words startle her. I see it in the way her shoulders stiffen before she turns around to face me. I watched her out of the corner of my eye as she exited the ladies' room and then stood near the bar checking her phone. Something on the small screen brought a bright smile to her face. I waited until she'd tucked the phone back into her black clutch purse before I approached her.

"What makes you say that?" She questions quietly.

"The way you look at him."

Her tongue slides over her bottom lip. "How do I look at him?"

"In a much different way than you look at me."

A blush blooms on the top of both of her cheeks. "I think that's understandable. I'm hoping you and I will work together. Charlie is a co-worker. He's a friend."

"Just a friend?" I step closer to her to allow a woman to pass behind me.

"We're a little more than friends but less than what you and Isadora are."

I swallow hard, frustration biting at me. "What does that mean? What do you think Isadora and I are?"

"In love," she says casually. "Charlie and I are nowhere near that level of seriousness."

This isn't a conversation I wanted to have in the middle of a restaurant while she's on a date with another man, but I won't allow her to carry around the false assumption that Isadora and I are still a couple.

"Is Isadora meeting you here for dinner?" She asks before I have a chance to say anything.

"Isadora and I broke up," I answer quickly. "I'm having dinner with someone else."

My words catch her by surprise. She looks down. I want her eyes on my face so I can read her expression. "I need to get back to my table and you shouldn't keep your date waiting, Julian."

"It's a business dinner, not a date."

Her head pops up. "It's a business dinner?"

I'm not about to share the fact that I'm meeting with an attorney who is going to negotiate Isadora's exit from not only my business but my life. Word moves quickly in this town so the fewer people who know that I've hired Chloe, the better.

"I need to see you tomorrow, Maya."

She stiffens. "See me?"

She feels it. There's no way in hell that she doesn't feel the same draw to me that I feel to her. The harmless flirting at the party the other night was one thing. The electric energy between us now is another. It's undeniable and considering the fact that she's having dinner with her boyfriend, it's dangerous.

I refuse to touch a woman who is devoted to another man, regardless of how badly I want to.

"I mentioned a business proposal at the launch party last week," I say it even though I know I'm playing with fire. Working with her will be sweet torture, but she deserves this chance. "I'd like to discuss that in detail with you."

I've kept a close eye on her career since we first met in Falon's studio. I've watched from afar as Maya has claimed a spot as an up and coming broker. She's worked hard to edge out more seasoned agents. She's managed a fair number of sales in a short period of time, which is virtually unheard of in Manhattan for a newly licensed broker. She's driven and determined.

Hiring someone with more experience to sell the residential suites in the new hotel would make sense on paper, but I need a fresh perspective and she can deliver that and more.

My intention was always to sit down and discuss this with Maya once the penthouse was staged. Her name never made it onto the guest list for the launch because that party was Isadora's brainchild. She hand chose the invitees and handled every aspect of the event from food to floral arrangements.

"Can you come by my office before noon? Does eleven work for you?"

Her eyes drop to her inner wrist and the hint of a tattoo beneath the band of her watch. I can't make out the script. All that's visible are curled lines of dark ink that dive under the black leather. "I'll be there. I should get back to the table."

She moves to step toward the entrance of the dining room when a server bumps into her from behind. She stumbles slightly, her hand darting out to steady herself.

I reach for her without thinking, my hands grabbing her to tug her close to my chest.

"Julian," she whispers as she steadies herself. "I…thank you. You saved me from falling."

"It was my pleasure." I run the pad of my thumb over the skin of her forearm. "Solely and completely my pleasure."

She looks up at me and her pink lips part as if she's going to stay something in response, but she doesn't. Instead, she sighs. It's the lightest sound, a sexy prelude to what her lover would hear when his fingers trace a path from her palm to her shoulder and then her neck before they glide over every inch of her body.

"I need to get back." She pulls away from me. "I've been gone too long."

I take a deep breath. "I'm right behind you, Maya. Lead the way."

She does and I follow, watching the sway of her ass beneath her red dress with every step she takes.

I've never anticipated a business meeting more than I do the one I have planned for tomorrow at eleven a.m. sharp.

Chapter 9

Maya

Julian Bishop is officially back on the market.

I spent most of last night tossing and turning in my bed thinking about that fact.

When I first saw him at the restaurant with the mysterious blonde, I didn't think much of it. There was no obvious affection between the two of them, although there wasn't an ounce between him and Isadora at the hotel launch party either.

Once he told me that they'd broken up, I couldn't think straight. I spent the next two hours listening to Charles tell me all about Charlie when he was a little kid. I couldn't repeat back one of those stories if my life depended on it.

I tried desperately to keep my eyes away from Julian. It didn't work until he raised a glass of wine in the air and tilted it in my direction.

I was mortified that I'd been caught staring at him. That was enough to keep my gaze trained on Charlie and his family until dinner was over.

"Maya, where are you? I come bearing gifts." I hear one of my favorite voices in the entire world float down the hallway toward where I'm standing in my bedroom.

I've already tried on three dresses and two skirts with four different white blouses, and it's not even nine a.m. yet. At this rate, I'll run through my entire closet before I make it to Julian's office.

"I'm in here, Fal," I call out. "I can't decide what to wear."

My best friend rounds the corner and stops in place in the doorway to my bedroom. Her curly brown hair is tied into a messy ponytail on the top of her head, her beautiful face is free of make-up, and she's wearing a pair of ripped jeans and a dark hoodie bearing the name of the world tour her husband launched late last year.

"Wear that." She gestures toward the cornflower blue sheath dress I'm wearing. "Your eyes match that perfectly, Maya. You look stunning."

I look down at the dress. It's a gift I gave myself for my birthday last year. I saw it on the runway during the Ella Kara show at New York Fashion Week. I was there with a client who insisted I tag along with her so we could talk about her apartment. I not only secured the listing during the show, but I also fell in love with the dress. Once the apartment sold, I tucked enough money away to buy the dress as soon as it hit the rack in the Ella Kara boutique. I've worn it dozens of times, and I doubt I'll ever tire of it.

"You think?" I twirl around on my bare feet. "Does it seem sophisticated enough?"

"It's understated." She steps forward to smooth her hand over the collar. "You're not showing too much skin, but it doesn't scream, 'I have zero personality' either. It's the dress. Wear it with your nude heels."

"Is it windy out? Do I need to wear a trench coat?"

"It's spring in New York. One minute it's hot as hell and the next the wind will lift you off your feet. I'd leave the trench at home today though." She tilts her head to study my face. "Your make up is on point today. So is your hair. What time did you get out of bed?"

I was up at the crack of dawn. I straightened my hair to within an inch of its life. I paired my smoky eye makeup with a touch of blush and a pale lipstick. It's striking enough to get me noticed, but not too much for a business meeting.

"Early," I confess. "I'm nervous, Fal. This is a big deal."

She tucks her keys into the front pocket of her jeans. I gave her a key to my apartment when I went back to San Francisco to visit my parents and my sister, Frannie, last fall. I would have asked Tilly to bring in my mail and water my plants, but she's been itching to move into my spare room since I bought this place. I have little doubt that she would have used my absence as an opportunity to move her stuff in and make herself at home.

I like living alone in a place that is bought and paid for by me. Technically, it will be paid for in twenty years after I've made every single one of my mortgage payments.

"Are you nervous about the actual meeting or about seeing Julian now that he's single?"

"You know how I feel about men who are newly single?" I adjust the sash on the dress. "A man needs at least two months to get his bearings."

"Not all men need that much time." She moves to sit on the edge of my bed. "I saw the chemistry between you two when he was in my studio. You told me on the phone that you felt it again last night at the restaurant."

I did tell her that. I called her once I was home to share the news that I was meeting with Julian today. She knows that I've been attracted to him for a long time. "A lot of couples break up and then get back together once they realize how much they miss each other. I don't want to get caught up in that again, Falon. I can't do it again."

She nods silently. Falon is well aware of the only time I've ever had my heart broken. That happened back in San Francisco and was a big part of the reason I ended up in New York City. Falling in love with a man who suddenly decides he's still in love with his ex is a situation I never want to find myself in again.

"Focus on the residential suites, Maya." Falon stands. "I brought coffee and breakfast sandwiches from Roasting Point. Let's eat and then I'll ride the subway with you down to the Bishop offices."

"This meeting could change my entire career." I smooth my hands over the skirt of my dress. "I know I'm ready, but I'm still scared. I don't want to fuck this up."

She reaches for my shoulders. "You're going to walk out of that office as the listing broker for those suites. Mark my words, Maya. The job is yours. I know it. I feel it."

Her pep talks have been the fuel that has propelled me through every career milestone to date. "I believe you. The job is mine."

If I can calm the butterflies in my stomach and keep the conversation focused on business, the job will be mine. I'm sure of it.

Chapter 10

Julian

"Why would I leave the organization?" Isadora doesn't glance up from where she's sitting in her usual perch behind her desk. "I built this company up just as you did. I have every right to be here."

I curse under my breath with an exasperated sigh. This discussion began via text last night near the end of my dinner meeting with Chloe. Isadora sent me a text asking me to meet her for a drink to discuss a contract related to the Bishop Hotel in Paris.

She'd received a call from our lawyer there yesterday morning and instead of asking me about it during office hours; she waited until the evening when she knew I'd be more prone to agree to a meeting over a drink.

I refused.

When she pressed, I shut her down with a quick response that I was at dinner.

She asked if I was with a woman. I answered honestly that I was and then the floodgates opened.

We spent much of last night in a heated text exchange about the breakdown of our relationship.

I suggested she think about finding a new job. She told me to fuck off. At that point, it was near two a.m., so I shut my phone off and tried to sleep.

"It's clear that co-existing here isn't going to be a viable option." I work to keep my tone even, calm and controlled. "I'm prepared to offer you a generous severance package, Isadora. I think it's best for both of us."

She lets out a huff of frustration. "I don't give a shit about what's best for you. I'm on my own now, aren't I? I have worked day and night for over three years to make this hotel chain what it is and now you're going to tell me that I have to give that up too? I won't. It's not happening, Julian."

"We can't continue to work together." I push a hand through my hair. "After last night, I think that's obvious."

"We've been broken up all of three days and you're already fucking someone else." Her voice raises to a level that I know will carry through the door and into the common space beyond where employees gather to drink coffee and brainstorm.

"Lower your voice." The words come out darker than I intend.

"Or what?" She pushes to her feet, her hands jumping to the middle of her chest. "Are you threatening me?"

"Of course not." I brush off her words with a wave of my hand in the air. "This is a personal matter that has no place in the office. I'm not going to discuss it with you here again."

"Do you know how painful it is to see you each day?" Her voice cracks. "I thought we'd spend the rest of our lives together. I thought we'd have a son and a daughter and raise them to take over the company."

I don't feel the pain she does. I've only felt the weight of the world being lifted from my shoulders since our relationship ended.

I was never satisfied with her. I may have tricked myself into believing I was based on the growth of the business, but personally, I was stifled.

"I'm sorry," I say softly. "I want you to be happy. I do, Isadora. I want you to find someone who can love you the way you deserve."

A sob bubbles up from her throat. "You can be that man, Julian. You can."

"I can't." I take a step toward her but stop myself. If I touch her to offer comfort, she'll misinterpret it as more. That can't happen.

"I have nowhere to go." She drops back into her chair. "I can't tell which way is up anymore."

I have no comforting words to offer her. I won't confuse her with anything that could be misconstrued as hope for a future between us.

"I'm going to take some time for myself." She looks up and into my face. "I'll go to Philadelphia to see some old friends this weekend. I'll catch a flight this afternoon."

I nod. I'm grateful for the brief reprieve, but the tension between us won't dissipate because she's leaving the state for a few days. "Stay as long as you need to. We'll discuss your future with Bishop when you return."

"You can't fire me, Julian," she says that with a chuckle. "I prepared my contract, remember? If I ever decide I want to leave, it's going to cost you."

I know and at this point, I'm willing to pay the price, however high it may be.

***

I have no doubt that Maya witnessed Isadora's spontaneous public display of affection outside the door to my office.

It caught me completely off guard.

After I walked out of Isadora's office to head to my own, she called from behind me. I turned just as I approached the open door of my office. That's the moment when Isadora decided to race toward me to throw herself into my arms. Her lips met mine before I was able to turn away.

Maya was standing directly in my line of sight, her hands on her hips and her left eyebrow cocked in surprise.

I ushered Isadora into the empty office next to mine and told her to keep her hands off of me in the future. Her response was another 'fuck you, Julian,' before she stormed out.

I took a second to control my agitation before I walked into my office to greet Maya.

"You have a little lipstick right there." Maya's finger slides over the left corner of her mouth.

I wipe the back of my hand over my lips.

"No, wait." She leans forward to circle her finger in the air near my mouth. "It's on that side. My left. Your right."

Fuck.

I reach for a tissue from the table next to the window and gingerly wipe the entire area around my mouth. I glance down at the red streak before I bunch the tissue into a ball and toss it in the wastebasket.

"Please have a seat, Maya." I nod toward the two leather chairs in front of my desk. "I'm sorry you had to witness that."

"Love is a complicated thing," she says as she lowers herself into one of the chairs. "I've never worked with someone I cared about before."

"Isadora was out of line." I take the seat next to her after I unbutton my black suit jacket. "She's having difficulty adjusting to our break up."

She doesn't acknowledge those words with a response. Instead, she gets right down to business. "I'm hopeful that you asked to meet me to discuss the residential suites in Bishop Chelsea."

I lean back in my chair. "I did. The board has been considering several brokers, including you."

"I'm the most digitally connected broker in this city," she goes on confidentially, "I have a large social media presence. That alone has helped me sell several properties in the past few months."

I'm well aware of that. I check her accounts on a daily basis. She engages her followers with professional quality photographs of the properties she's listed mixed in with personal images of her life in New York. She has a pulse on the future of real estate, which is why I pushed the board into giving her this chance.

I may have the final say but having the board's backing is essential on a project of this magnitude. The residential suites in Bishop Chelsea are an experiment of sorts. If they sell quickly and at the price I want, I expect to incorporate residences in every future hotel we launch.

"Your reputation precedes you." I smile. "I'm prepared to offer you the exclusive listing, Maya."

"You are?" She slides forward in her chair, her hands darting to her lap. "Thank you so much. Oh my god, thank you."

"There's one condition." I inch forward until my knees are almost brushing against hers.

"Of course." Her gaze trails over my body, stopping once her eyes meet mine. "What's the condition?"

That you have dinner with me. At my place, tonight. Clothing optional.

Those words dance on the tip of my tongue, but I push them back. I have no fucking idea how I'm going to work with this woman. I don't understand why Charlie Warton deserves her attention.

"The condition, Julian?" Her voice is soft. "Please tell me what it is."

"You have thirty days to sell the penthouse, Maya."

Her brow bunches in confusion. "Thirty days to sell the penthouse?"

"I want that sold in thirty days. If you can accomplish that, the remaining eleven units are yours to sell. If you can't, I'll find another broker."

It's a near-impossible task, but the board insisted and I agreed. I may want Maya in my bed, but I'm not going to allow my better judgment to be clouded by my selfish needs.

Those residences have to be sold quickly and as close to list price as possible.

"You have a deal." She holds out her delicate hand in the air between us.

I take it in mine. "I'll have legal prepare the contract, Maya. Welcome onboard."

Chapter 11

Maya

"If anyone else came to me with this deal in hand, I'd scream at them." Anne looks up from the stack of papers I gave her just now.

It's the contract I signed with Bishop. I gave it to Anne two days ago when Bishop's legal team sent it to me via courier. She perused it before handing it over to Lillian, the head of legal at Carvel Properties. She went over it carefully at the same time, my lawyer, Zoe Beck, did.

It got everyone's approval, so I signed on the dotted line an hour ago. I had a copy made for Anne for her records. Zoe is holding onto my signed copy.

"You know that I'm going to sell that penthouse," I try to sound more confident than I feel. I'm fully aware of the mountain that I'm facing. The penthouse is priced high and the list of buyers willing to part with more than twenty million dollars is short and tapped out at this point.

We hit most of our overseas contacts up just six weeks ago when Dax was desperate for a buyer for a luxury condo he'd been trying to sell for more than three months.

My listing will appeal to more of our high-end clients simply because they are buying a piece of New York history. Bishop is offering a full floor penthouse with panoramic views of the entire city and beyond. That alone isn't history making, but the fact that it's the first ever Bishop Hotel residence to be sold is. I'm going to play up that fact because many wealthy buyers want to lay claim to something that no one has before them.

"We need to schedule a broker's open house." Anne grabs her cell phone from her desk. "I'm thinking Thursday night."

"I'm already on it." I laugh. "Jen is handling the caterer and the flowers. I've got Dan working on the e-invites for that. I've narrowed the list down to the brokers I know have contacts who would be interested in a residence inside of a hotel. My list is just over one hundred at this point."

"Maya." Anne pivots on her heel to face me. "What the hell? You're way ahead of me on this."

I have to be. The clock is officially ticking on my thirty day trial period. I had my new assistant, Jen, working on the broker open house an hour after I hired her. That happened the afternoon of my meeting with Julian.

Jen worked as a rental agent here at Carvel when I did. She left after the birth of her first child and when we met for our regular monthly lunch three weeks ago, she expressed an interest in getting back into the workforce part-time. I called her to offer her a job after I left Julian's office.

I'm borrowing Anne's assistant to help me with the e-invites because she offered his services if I ever needed them. I'll gift him with a bottle of wine to thank him for pitching in.

This listing is costing me a pretty penny, but I have enough in my business account to cover the expenses and I have an accountant who works financial magic like a wizard. In real estate, you have to spend money to make money to get ahead.

"I'm heading over to the hotel now to do a walk through and get a feel for the space. Do you want to come with me?" I offer because it's the right thing to do. I want and need Anne's help with this, even though it's my listing.

"I can't." She looks up at the large circular clock hanging on her office wall. "I have a meeting in thirty."

Even though I saw the penthouse just a few days ago, I want to revisit to get a better feeling for the space. Julian had his assistant take me over to it after our meeting. He said he would have liked to have given me the grand tour himself, but he had a pressing matter to deal with.

I didn't mind. I needed the time to catch my breath after witnessing that kiss between him and Isadora. He didn't seem like a willing participant but it still shook me to see the two of them in a lip lock after he'd confessed just the night before that they'd broken up.

"You're going to make me proud, Maya." Anne pulls me into a quick embrace. "You remind me of myself at your age."

I smile at that. I know I'll make her proud. I have every intention of selling that penthouse before the deadline. I have exactly thirty days to make it happen.

***

"I didn't expect to see you here, Julian."

He turns instantly from where he's standing facing the wall of windows that overlooks west Manhattan and the now setting sun. His gaze rakes me from head-to-toe.

I'm dressed in a black pinstriped pencil skirt and a yellow blouse. I pinned my hair up today. His eyes linger on my neck.

He looks dashing in his navy blue three-piece suit and white shirt. A week ago I would have told him how handsome he is, but now that feels out of place. I've already decided that the harmless flirting that took place at the launch party and the restaurant has to stop.

Not only is he my client, but he's in the middle of a breakup, or maybe it's a non-break up, with Isadora. Getting involved with him would spell trouble for me and my career.

"I could say the same for you, Maya." His voice is gruff and deep. I could seriously get off just hearing the man talk dirty to me.

So much for keeping my mind on business.

"I'm officially on board to sell this space." I smile as I survey the tastefully decorated living room. "I need to get to know every inch of it."

"Every inch," he repeats in little more than a whisper as he tilts his head to the left to study me. "I received the signed contract before I left my office. I think we should celebrate."

I turn to look toward the chef's kitchen. "I think any and all celebrations should take place once the penthouse is sold."

I can hear and sense him moving behind me. "You just landed the biggest listing of your career. Surely a drink is in order."

I turn quickly to face him. The toes of his shoes are almost touching mine. The man smells incredible. His body is close enough that a single small movement of my hand and I'd feel the muscle of his bicep. "I don't think that's a good idea, Julian."

His full lips ease into a smile. "I beg to differ, Maya."

Jesus, he's gorgeous. This is exactly my type. Everything about him is my type including his ability to make me wet just from his mere presence.

"I don't think it's wise."

"Why not?" He steps even closer, closing the small gap that was between us.

The air in the vast space feels instantly thick and threaded with need. I tell myself to take a step back but my black stilettos stay firmly planted on the area rug beneath them.

"We work together," I say softly. "You have a girlfriend."

He reaches forward to adjust the collar of my blouse. I don't move. My breath stops as my heart stutters. "I don't have a girlfriend, but you have a Charlie."

I don't have a Charlie. I haven't spoken to him since the dinner at the restaurant with his dad and stepmom. Charlie ushered me into a taxi on the street that night because he had to stay to discuss something with his father. I didn't complain. I was happy to ride home alone.

I've been meaning to talk to him but between meeting with his dad's attorney regarding the listing of Charles and Hazel's apartment and the excitement surrounding this contract with Bishop Hotels, my time hasn't been my own.

"I'm not asking you out on a date, Maya," he clarifies as his breath skips over my cheek. "This is strictly a drink between business associates. Nothing more."

Nothing more.

I want more.

I ignore the temptation to say that. "Just a drink?"

"One drink," he whispers. "We'll toast to your impending success."

I know how important it is to keep a client happy. I wouldn't hesitate if any other client invited me out for a drink. "One drink it is."

He looks down at the large silver watch on his wrist. "I'll leave you here to get better acquainted with the space. I'll meet you downstairs in the hotel bar in an hour."

"An hour," I repeat back. "I'll see you then, Julian."

Unable to take my gaze off of him, I watch as he turns and walks to the corridor that leads to the private elevator.

I suck in a deep, audible breath once I'm sure he's out of earshot.

I signed the biggest contract of my career and I'm having a drink with Julian Bishop. This is quickly becoming one of the best days of my life.

Chapter 12

Julian

My hunger for Maya is insatiable. I tried to quiet it when I was standing in front of her in the penthouse. I wanted to grab her and push her against the window so I could claim her mouth with mine. I had a fleeting vision of turning her around and eating her from behind while she breathed against the windows, with the striking views of the city as our backdrop.

Inviting her for a drink was a selfish move. I knew she'd struggle to say no, even though she tried to resist.

She's in a relationship with a man who has a brilliant legal mind. He has the one thing I want and that's her. I've seen them together. Their connection is as void of passion as mine was with Isadora.

I watch her exit the elevator and enter the lobby of the hotel. She has a trench coat strung over her forearm, and a small purse slung over her shoulder. She looks nervous, apprehensive.

I stand from where I've been waiting next to the bar. It's shortly past six, so the crowd is thin. Business will pick up as the night wears on.

We hold back several rooms every night from the reservation list for the patrons of the bar who decide they want to take their private party to a room. I don't judge what the people who stay in my hotels do. If they use the well-appointed rooms for random hook-ups, I'm more than happy to take a full night's fee from them.

There may be cheaper places to have a nameless fuck in this city, but when the urge strikes, a good bargain is the last thing on a person's mind.

She spots me as her eyes scan the dimly lit bar. I wave for good measure and plaster a genuine smile on my face.

That brings a grin to her lips. She's a breathtaking woman.

When I first spotted her in Falon's studio, I was drawn to her like a moth to a flame. My feet carried me straight to her and like a caveman, I was tempted to throw her over my shoulder and carry her out of there.

I've never stopped thinking about her and as I've worked hard to build my company's brand and open new locations, she's maneuvered her way through her career and a number of short-term relationships.

Envy was always there when I thought of her with other men, but I'd made a choice. I put my business before everything including my desire to pursue her.

"Julian," she says my name as she approaches. "I'm sorry I'm late."

I lost track of time. I used the hour to answer emails and make notes regarding a meeting I'll have in the days to come with the head of our Paris office. The hotel that's currently under construction there isn't without its share of hiccups, but it's on track and set to open before the end of the year.

"What can I get you?" I tap the top of the bar to signal the bartender. She tried to make small talk when I first sat down, unaware that I'm her boss. When I finally introduced myself her demeanor shifted from overly friendly to cautiously casual.

"I'll have a dirty martini."

It's too dark to see the blush on her cheeks, but the look in her eyes tells me it's there.

"Two dirty martinis," I tell the bartender before I point at an empty table in the corner. "We're settling over there."

She nods as she gives Maya the once over before she starts on our drinks.

"The bar is as beautiful as every other part of this hotel." Maya's gaze slides over the details of the space as we take our seats. "Did your sister do the interior design for the entire hotel?"

She didn't. I asked Brynn to come on board to lend a hand for the residential suites. I trust her eye, and her degree in design, but I wanted a more refined aesthetic for the public areas. "Brynn took care of the design for the residences."

"Those are stunning." She folds her coat over the back of the chair next to her before she places her purse on the seat. "She's very talented."

"That she is." I nod, as I sit across from her. "If you'd like to speak with her regarding any of the design elements, my assistant can arrange that."

She catches my gaze over the lit candle in the middle of the table. The light it's casting makes her look like an angel.

"Do you have questions for me regarding the penthouse, Maya?" I lean back, resting my hand on the back of the chair where she placed her coat. "I'm here to help."

Her mouth curves. "Not at the moment, but if I think of any, it would be good to have your direct number so I can call you."

Progress. That's what I see this as. She wants my number and frankly, I don't give a shit if it's because she intends to call me to ask me about the ventilation system in the penthouse or if it's to have phone sex with me.

I tug my phone from the inner pocket of my suit jacket and shoot her a quick text.

Her phone chimes in her purse. "Did you just text me?"

"I did." I stop when the bartender approaches with our drinks.

"Thank you." Maya smiles brightly at the woman as she slides her martini onto the table.

I wait until she's walked away before I sample the drink. It's not as thirst quenching as the aged whiskey I had earlier, but it's a decent martini. "I should have given you my direct line the other day."

"I don't mind talking to your assistant." She takes a sip of her drink and swallows slowly. "She's a lovely woman."

She is. I value everyone who works for me. Their paychecks and benefit packages reflect that.

"I have a question for you."

She leans her elbow on the table. "I'm all ears."

No, she's not. She's all lush curves and soft skin. She's full lips and perfumed perfection. I shift in my chair trying to edge away from the desire that is causing my cock to swell.

"Why did you choose real estate as a career?"

She takes another drink before she considers her answer. I watch her long eyelashes bat as she surveys the room. "I knew early on that I was great at selling things. First, it was clothing, then cars and finally, after college, homes."

"You're a born salesperson?" I question with a grin.

"Something like that." She laughs. "I understand how to make people comfortable in their decision to make a purchase. That's essentially what real estate is. I'm there to hold their hand and lead them in the right direction."

I look down at her hand. Her fingernails are manicured and painted a soft pink. A watch is covering her wrist again. I instantly wonder about that tattoo I caught a glimpse of the other night.

"Why are you in the hotel business?"

"I inherited it," I answer honestly. "My grandfather founded Bishop Hotels. My father followed the same career path as you, so that left me to take over where my grandfather left off."

"It was a small operation when you took over." She tips her martini glass toward me. "You've taken it internationally."

I smile. I like that she knows that. She's done her research.

"I did," I say simply.

The silence that follows is punctuated with only the beating of my heart. I stare at her across the table as her gaze stays locked on mine. I'd envisioned a night like this every time she crossed my mind, yet now, that it's happening I'm restrained because of her commitment to Warton Jr.

"How serious are things between you and Charlie?" The question comes out because the need to know is too strong.

"Charlie?" She parrots his name back to me and fuck if it doesn't make me hate the name. I don't want to hear her say it. I don't want her to say any man's name but mine.

"You were having dinner with his parents the other night. I may be rusty on dating etiquette, but I remember that being the sign of something serious."

"It's not like that." She sighs heavily. "There's nothing serious between us. We haven't even…"

Kissed? Fucked? What?

"Charlie and I are friends," she qualifies. "We've been on a few dates."

"If Charlie and you weren't friends, would have dinner with me?"

She flicks her tongue over her bottom lip. "A dinner that didn't include business?"

"A date," I say clearly. "If Charlie was no longer in the picture, would you agree to go on a date with me, Maya?"

She shakes her head. "No, I wouldn't."

Chapter 13

Maya

It's obvious immediately that Julian wasn't expecting me to say no to his question about going on a date with him if Charlie wasn't in my life.

I could very easily explain that I have zero plans to go on another date with Charlie, but I don't. It's not Julian's business. Besides, he's the one who had his ex-girlfriend's lipstick all over his mouth the other day.

"No?" He perks his left brow. "Have I misread the energy between us, Maya?"

It would be virtually impossible to do that. Even now, with a small table separating us, the desire is palpable. I know he wants me. I feel it. He can feel that I want him too.

I won't act on it though. I can't.

"I'm very attracted to you," I confess before I swallow another gulp of my martini. "I think I made that clear the first time we met."

"I believe you could tell that the feeling was mutual, then and now."

I feel a shiver inch down my spine with his words. It's not that I have any doubt that he wants me. Hearing him say it takes it to a new level.

"I have a hard rule about dating men who recently broke up with a lover."

His gaze narrows. "Why is that?"

I won't get into the finer details about how my heart was broken and trampled on back in San Francisco. I've put that in my past, but the lingering pain of that was almost too much to bear. I remember it and never want to experience it again. Hence the reason I've sworn off men who are still on their ex-girlfriend's radar.

"Many couples who break up get back together." I cross my legs under the table. "I don't want to get caught up in the middle of that."

"I take it you have experience with that?" he questions as he sips on his drink. "You were involved with a man who left you for his ex?"

Bingo. Way to hit the nail on the head, Julian.

"It happened. It hurt, so I avoid it now," I state simply.

"Isadora and I are done." He finishes his drink in one swallow. "I assure you that if we dated, there is zero risk of my getting back together with her."

That may be true, but judging by the show Isadora put on the other day at his office, there's a reasonably high risk that she'll attack me with whatever is within arm's reach if she hears that I'm dating her boss and ex-lover.

"You two work together," I point out with a tap of my fingers on the tabletop. "I essentially work for you at the moment. That's a triangle to me, and I hate triangles."

He doesn't respond. He's considering my words. I can tell by the way his eyes are darting over my face.

"Beyond that, I don't think it's wise for me to sleep with a client," I stop to correct myself with a hand over my eyes. "Oh gosh. No. I used the wrong word. I meant date a client."

I lower my hand to find him staring intently at me. "You did use the wrong word, Maya. We wouldn't sleep together. I can guarantee that if I were ever fortunate enough to have you in my bed, you wouldn't sleep a wink."

We'd fuck. We'd fuck for hours. I know it. I feel it.

I shift in my chair, uncrossing my legs because the friction is causing my panties to rub against the smooth skin of my pussy. I need to go home so I can touch myself before I implode right here in front of him.

"Forgive me if that was out of line." He reaches across the table to cover my hand with his. "I'll say this once and leave it at that. I want you, Maya. If your rules ever change, you know where to find me."

With that, he gets up, buttons his suit jacket and walks out of the bar.

Holy shit.

What the hell just happened? Is this a dream or did Julian Bishop just tell me that he's mine to fuck whenever I want?

***

I take off the skirt and blouse that I was wearing when I saw Julian and I stand in my bedroom in just my panties and bra.

I left the bar shortly after he did. I ran out to the street not sure of what I'd say if I did catch up with him, but by the time I made it to the entrance of the hotel, he was getting in the back of a taxi.

My need for him was strong in that moment. It overpowered my common sense. If I would have approached the taxi before it pulled into traffic, he would have seen my desire to go home with him.

Instead, I stood silently and watched it drive away before I waved to the hotel doorman so he could flag me down a taxi too.

I fish in my purse for my phone when I hear the familiar chime signaling an incoming message.

I swipe my thumb over the phone's screen to read the text.

There was an emergency at the clinic so I just read your message about the penthouse job now. Holy crap, Maya! I'm so proud of you. I'll call you tomorrow!

I immediately type back a response to Tilly.
Thank you, sis. Love you.

After I press send, I scroll down to another unread message. This one is from a New York number I don't immediately recognize. It's a familiar part of my world. I get dozens of messages every day from prospective buyers and sellers.

You're the most beautiful woman I've ever met, Maya. Use this number at any time for ANY reason.

I check the timestamp on the message. It was sent when I was in the hotel bar.

Julian. It's Julian's private cell number.

I enter it into my contact list. My thumb hovers over the screen.

Finally, I type out a message.

Thank you for the drink, Julian.

His response comes quickly.

It was my pleasure.

His pleasure. It's what I think about as I crawl into bed, tuck my hand in my panties and fall asleep dreaming about what it would have been like to go home with him tonight.

Chapter 14

Julian

"Do you want my advice, Julian?"

I scrub my hand over my face. I'm paying her for her advice so the answer to that question should be clear. "Of course, I do, Chloe."

She stands in front of my desk. "As I told you on the phone, Isadora has retained counsel to represent her interest in the company. She has no intention of quitting. Her attorney stressed that point when she called me."

I'm not fucking surprised. Isadora's life has been consumed by this job for the past three-and-a-half years. She has no family to speak of. Bishop Hotels and our relationship are all she had. If she can't have one, she'll fight tooth and nail to hold fast to the other.

"Get to the advice part."

"A quick question first." Her hand smooths her messy bun. It's obvious she's put in a full day at her office. I asked her to meet me at mine after I'd left Maya at the bar. I don't need the prying and curious eyes of my employees around to witness this meeting. Too many of them are loyal to Isadora.

Although Isadora is aware that I've brought Chloe on to help negotiate her severance, she doesn't need the reminder of it being thrown in her face when she comes back to the office. She requested an extended leave of absence, which I readily agreed to. That won't last forever though.

"What's the question?" My patience is waning. I'm frustrated and tired.

"Has Isadora ever mentioned wanting to work for another company?"

I cock both brows in answer to that. It's a ridiculous question. "What do you think?"

"I think that if you can find her a better job than the one she has here, that she'll gladly take a substantial offer to nullify her contract with Bishop Hotels."

"Are you pulling that idea out of thin air or is this coming from Isadora's attorney?"

"I'm speaking from experience." She drops into one of the chairs in front of my desk. "I've had several clients in the past who were dead set against leaving their posts, but as soon as a more attractive offer was presented at a different company, they left the job they claimed to love."

It's difficult for me to imagine Isadora wanting to work anywhere but here.

"Where did Isadora work before you hired her?"

"At a firm in Philadelphia." I hang my head. "We met while I was there scouting for a new location."

"Would she be interested in going back?"

I shake my head. "Hell, no. She hated that job."

"Fine." She stands again. "I'm wiped out, Julian. I'm heading home. Give some thought to what we just talked about. If Isadora has a dream job beyond Bishop, your problem might be solved."

I nod. She needs to find a different approach to deal with Isadora. I need to get some sleep.

***

"As you can all see, this is an exquisite property with views that are priceless," Maya speaks clearly to the gathered crowd. "One of the reasons I wanted you all here was so you could witness the sun setting from this vantage point."

Almost every head turns in the direction of the west facing windows.

"Imagine your clients eating dinner to that view every night and bear in mind that the master bedroom faces east so they'll be greeted with sunrises that are equally as breathtaking."

I inch closer hoping to catch a glimpse of her.

"I'm available to answer any questions you have about the property and the hotel amenities." She lowers her voice slightly. "Please enjoy the beverages and snacks. Have a look around and consider which of your clients are going to want to call this place home."

The crowd of people starts to thin as some wander the corridor that leads to the bedrooms while others move to explore the other wing of the penthouse where the library and private gym are located.

Even though she didn't invite me to the broker's open house, I wanted to be present. Not to watch her every move over her shoulder, but to get a sense of the interest.

I finally see her standing next to a man with red hair. She's talking to him, her eyes trained on his face.

She's dressed in a simple black dress and heels. Her hair is falling loosely around her face. She may look younger than her twenty-five-years, but her voice is confident, her presence strong.

I walk toward her, slowing as I near her.

"I can meet you and your client here at noon sharp tomorrow, Rob." She reaches to touch his forearm through his suit jacket. "I already have two other showings lined up, so please stress to your client how time sensitive it is. If she wants the apartment, she'll need to be here for that appointment."

"I'll have her here, Maya." He smiles down at her. "We'll be here at noon. Maybe the two of us can grab a bite after?"

"Maya," I say her name to interrupt Rob's attempt to secure a lunch date with her. If I don't have a shot, I'm going to make damn sure this guy doesn't either.

"Julian?" Maya peeks past Rob's shoulder to look at me. "I didn't know you'd be here."

"Julian Bishop?" Rob turns to face me. He's as unfamiliar to me as virtually every face in this apartment. If I had given the listing to my father as the board wanted, I doubt he would have had a broker's open house. He would have been hell bent on selling this penthouse on his own.

I intentionally didn't go with my dad's firm because I made a promise to my grandfather that I'd never involve my dad in the business.

His ego is his biggest competitor and it's cost him more business than he'd ever admit.

"Julian, this is Rob Norton." Maya once again touches Rob's arm. "Rob works with me at Carvel."

I shake his hand. "It's good to meet you, Rob."

"You as well." He finally drops my hand. "I've long admired your work, sir. Your branding for your hotels is on point."

I have a stellar marketing department to thank for that, but I'll take credit. "Thanks, Rob."

"I should call the client we talked about, Maya." He reaches to squeeze her hand. "I'll meet you here at noon."

She nods as he wanders off with his phone in his palm.

"Can I get you a drink?" Maya motions toward the kitchen were a man dressed in a tuxedo is serving glasses of champagne on a tray.

"No, but thank you." I take a moment to look around the room. "I'm impressed. You've brought out a lot of people, Maya."

"They all work for Carvel." She rests her hip against the wall. "Every agent and broker has their list of contacts, so they're all putting out feelers to see if they have interested buyers."

I want her to sell the penthouse not only because of the monetary benefit to Bishop Hotels but for the sole reason that she deserves a chance to shine.

"I'd like to meet with you early tomorrow afternoon to talk about those brochures you had printed that are now in every room of all the Bishop hotels in this city. It's a brilliant approach to sell the penthouse."

I was in awe when one was placed on my desk earlier today. It's a tasteful brochure with vivid images of the interior of the penthouse and a brief rundown of all the benefits of owning it. Her contact details are front and center along with photo credits to Falon Shaw.

I have no idea when she managed to pull it all together. I do know that she spoke to the director of marketing who gave her the go-ahead to distribute the brochures to our hotels in Manhattan.

"Thank you." She runs her finger over her bottom lip. "Let me guess. You want to meet me right after the private showing I have with Rob and his client. You overhead our conversation, didn't you?"

"One o'clock in the restaurant downstairs, Maya. I'll be the one with the smile on my face."

"For the record, I wasn't going to have lunch with him."

I lean forward to whisper against the shell of her ear. "For the record, you smell incredible."

That brings a bubble of laughter from deep within her. "Flirt."

"Enjoy your evening, Maya." I inch back so I can look into her eyes.

"My rules haven't changed, Julian."

My jaw twitches as I fight the urge to kiss her. "Yet, Maya. Your rules haven't changed, yet."

She turns away from me as someone calls her name from the kitchen. "I need to get back to work. I'll see you tomorrow."

"Tomorrow, it is," I reply as she walks away without looking back.

Chapter 15

Maya

I look across the penthouse to the man standing near the corridor that leads in from the private elevator. I can't believe my eyes.

"Charlie?" I turn to where he's standing next to me. "I don't know how you pulled this off, but I'm forever grateful."

He smiles softly, his index finger nudging his glasses up his nose. "We're friends, right?"

I nod. We are. We established that last night during a text exchange.

Charlie sent me a text after the broker's open house to congratulate me on its success. I didn't know he was there, but he said he was and that he'd met someone. It's a woman who works in accounting. She tagged along with one of the sales agents to get a glimpse of the penthouse.

She's new, blonde and much more his type than I'll ever be.

They hit it off, and he wanted to let me down easy.

He did. He was kind, gentle and assured me that our breakup, as he called it, wouldn't impact my contract with his dad to sell his place.

I fell asleep relieved that I didn't have to be the one to tell him that it was over.

"Of course, we're friends."

"I'm the kind of guy who wants his friends to succeed." His voice lightens. "I asked my other friends if they knew anyone who would be interested in living here. One of them said he had someone in mind, so that's why I brought that guy over there. He's a pretty big deal, Maya. I'm sure that he could pay cash for this place and it wouldn't put a dent in his bank account."

I'm sure of that too.

"So Trey Hale is a friend of a friend?" I question him.

"Who knew that one of my friends from high school knows the best pitcher in the league?" He laughs. "I'm sorry we just showed up, but Anne said your showing at noon would be over, so we came right down. Trey's anxious to see the place."

I glance down at my phone. It's almost one.

"I need to send a very quick text message and then I can give him the grand tour. Is he working with an agent or broker?"

"No." Charlie shakes his head. "This is the first property he's looked at. On the way over he said he just wants a place to hang his hat, or in his case, baseball cap."

I laugh as I type out a text to Julian telling him that I have to skip our lunch meeting.

"I have a good feeling about this, Maya." Charlie rests his hand on the middle of my back as we make our way toward Trey. "Today may be the day you sell this place."

***

"The thing I like best about this place is the fact that I can order up room service whenever I damn well please." Trey takes a seat at one of the stools next to the massive kitchen island. "It's a hell of a lot of space for one guy, but it's a good investment, right?"

He directs that question at Charlie who answers in a heartbeat. "Real estate in Manhattan is always a solid investment, Trey."

"I like it." He stares at the imported granite countertops. "I could throw some wicked parties in here."

He could have three hundred people in here and they'd never bump into each other. "Do you have any questions for me?"

He finally turns to look at me. He's handsome. It's just one of the reasons he's such a recognizable face in the city. "Are you single?"

Jesus. Seriously? I know his reputation, but I assumed with Charlie standing next to me, that he'd keep his libido in check.

"Questions about the property," I stress. "I can show you both the rooftop terrace if you're not afraid of a little wind and rain."

Trey scratches the beginnings of a beard that has settled on his chin. "I'm genuinely curious, Maya. Are you seeing anyone?"

"I… the thing is that I don't discuss my personal life at work." I fumble through that. "I have another private showing soon so if you'd like to have one last look around before we finish up; please feel free to do that."

"What time are you done for the day?" Trey stands and shoves his hands into the front pocket of his jeans. He takes his time looking me over, which makes me wish I had worn anything but this sleeveless blue blouse and black skirt.

"Maya's schedule is booked solid."

I hear Julian's voice from behind me just as Trey's expression shifts.

"Who are you?" he asks as he cocks his head to the side.

Julian brushes past me with his hand extended. "Julian Bishop. I own the hotel. It's good to meet you."

"You too." Trey takes his hand for a short shake before he turns back to me. "I'm taking off, Maya, but I have your number. I'll give this place some thought and then I'll be in touch."

I nod. "It was good to meet you, Trey."

He eyes me up one last time. "I'll call you before the end of the week."

As he starts to walk away, I turn to Charlie and mouth a quick '*thank you*' before he takes off on Trey's heel.

"Why did you come up here?" I ask the question to Julian's back. I know he's looking at something on his phone's screen, but irritation is nipping at my last nerve. "I texted you to tell you I had another showing, Julian. You know that prospective buyers can be overwhelmed if too many people are hovering around them."

He turns to face me. "I have a meeting, Maya. It can't wait. We'll need to discuss this later."

"I need you to trust me to sell this place." I stop him when I grab his forearm as he brushes past me.

He looks down at my hand before he places his over it. "I trust you. This has nothing to do with that."

"I'm just having trouble understanding why you suddenly made an appearance."

"I saw Trey walk into the lobby with Charlie." He squeezes my hand. "I'm a baseball fan. I wanted to meet the man who won the series for New York."

I can't tell if he's being genuine or not. "You like baseball?"

"I have season tickets." He traces his fingertip in a lazy circle over the top of my hand. "I am curious about something though. Why didn't Charlie step in when Trey was hitting on you?"

"Charlie knows I can take care of myself."

"I'm sure he does." He sighs deeply. "Let me rephrase my question. Explain to me why neither of you pointed out to Trey that you're dating."

"We're not." I tug my hand free of his. "Charlie met someone else."

"So it's over between you two?" He smiles widely. "That's good to know."

"It doesn't change my rules, Julian." I rub the back of my neck. "I still won't go on a date with you."

"I know, Maya." He leans down until his lips are almost touching mine. "I won't push you to break your rules. I'll only remind you that I'm available if you ever feel the urge to break them."

Chapter 16

Maya

The number one rule in real estate is *always keep your client happy*, and since the clock is ticking away at a fast pace on my thirty days, I do the only thing I can. I call Julian Bishop.

I haven't seen the man in two days. The last time was when he walked out of this penthouse after the showing I had with Trey Hale. That amounted to a phone call from his financial advisor telling me that Trey's budget for an apartment is only a fraction of the price of the penthouse. I told him I'd be in touch as soon as the other residences in the hotel hit the market. He was overjoyed to hear that.

A potential future sale is always good.

Julian answers on the second ring. "Maya. To what do I owe this pleasure?"

I've imagined phone sex with him and now that I hear the rough timbre of his voice over the phone, I know it would be better than some actual sex I've had in my life.

"I have a question," I say softly. "It's more a favor, I suppose."

"Tell me what it is."

I hesitate only briefly. I wouldn't make this call unless I felt forced to do it, especially after the fact that I essentially told him less than forty-eight hours ago that I didn't want him showing up during my listing appointments.

"I'm showing the penthouse and there's a couple here who would like to meet you." I glance over at Tom and Irene Clarkson, the retired couple who contacted me earlier today after seeing the brochure in their hotel room detailing the penthouse residence. They were eager to see the space, so I arranged to meet them here ten minutes ago. Now, they're insisting on a face-to-face with Julian. "I'm sorry to bother you with this. I know how busy you are."

"I'll be right there." With those words, the call ends and my heartbeat steps up to a thrumming beat inside my chest.

***

"Do you think there's enough space for a dance party?" Irene twirls in place in the center of the open concept living and dining room area. "Tom and I love to dance."

"There's more than enough room, dear." Tom moves to stand next to his wife. "Let's give it a try, shall we?"

I love this. Seeing two people this much in love always warms my heart. They've held hands through most of the tour I just gave them of the penthouse. They spoke lovingly about their three children and four grandchildren when they viewed the bedrooms.

Purchasing a property in New York is something they've long considered, and now that their oldest son is living here with his family, they feel the time is right to make the move.

"I can turn on some music," I offer. I've tried to keep them occupied with small talk about the hotel amenities while we wait for Julian to arrive.

"Sinatra is our favorite." Tom tosses me a wink.

I scroll through the music app on my phone until I find a ballad. I turn up the volume, and the song starts just as Tom reaches to tug his wife into his arms.

They move together seamlessly, their bodies obviously so familiar with one another that they can anticipate the other's moves before they happen. I watch spellbound, the wishful parts of me hopeful that one day I'll have a connection as intense and natural as this.

The song ends and another begins. This one is even more soulful. Irene closes her eyes as she rests her head against her husband's chest.

I almost jump out of my skin when I feel the light tap of a hand on my shoulder. "May I have this dance?"

I smile as I cock my head to look and into Julian's face. "You want to dance?"

"Don't you? How inspiring are those two?" He gestures to Tom and Irene who are lost in a world of their own.

Before I have a chance to answer, Julian is sliding off his suit jacket. He places it over the back of a leather sofa before he sets to work removing his silver and sapphire cufflinks. Those get placed on a small wooden table next to the sofa.

I watch intently as he pushes the sleeves of his white dress shirt to his elbows revealing toned, thick forearms.

"I need to get comfortable to dance." He extends a hand to me. "Do you want to take off anything before we get started?"

I glance down at the short black dress and strappy heels I'm wearing. "I'm good."

Another slow song begins and as the magical sound of Sinatra's voice fills the air, I step into Julian's arms.

"You should call me over to dance during every listing appointment you have," he whispers those words as he leads me over the hardwood floor. "You're a wonderful dancer, Maya."

He's kind. He's an incredible dancer. Sure of each step, his touch gentle enough to guide me, yet firm enough to command my body to follow his.

I'm pressed against his chest. My left hand is resting on his shoulder, while the right is cupped tenderly in his palm. This is the closest I've ever been to him. I feel every ridge of his firm chest and toned stomach beneath his white dress shirt. I know he's hard. He has to know I'm aroused.

"You two are a sight," Irene says as she glances at us. "Who do they remind you of, Tom?"

"Us, my darling." He kisses her cheek. "They remind me of us the very first time I asked you to dance."

Chapter 17

Julian

As the music fades, Maya steps away from me and I feel a sense of loss that is hard to explain. I've never felt anything near what I'm feeling for her and touching her that way, as innocent as it was, left my body twisted with need.

I'm erect, wanting and tired of the craving ache that has become a normal part of my life whenever she's near me.

"This is Irene and Tom Clarkson." Maya steps closer to the older couple she asked me here to meet. "They are staying at Bishop Tribeca and noticed the brochure."

I shake both of their hands firmly. "It's good to meet you both. How are you enjoying your stay?"

"The hotel is one of the best we've ever stayed in." Tom smiles as he wraps his arm around his wife's shoulders. "We want something more permanent now that our son is living here. Tell us about the neighborhood."

It's a question he easily could have asked Maya, but he didn't. He wanted a face-to-face with me for the simple reason that this property costs a fortune and if he's going to invest his hard earned money in it, he wants to know the owner.

I get that. I would do the very same if I were standing in his shoes.

"You're not going to see as much tourist traffic here in Chelsea as you would in other areas." I walk toward the wall of windows that overlook the Hudson River. I doubt anyone has noticed my now semi-hard cock pressing against the fabric of my navy trousers, but I need it to calm down before I walk out of here. "The restaurants in the neighborhood are great. They're not as stellar as our offering downstairs, but you can sample a different dish every night for a year within a two block radius."

"The views are what grabbed us when we saw the brochure." Tom moves to stand next to me. "This is what a person moves to New York for. That and their family, of course."

I chuckle. "It's the ideal space to host family gatherings. It's a place where memories can be built for generations to come."

"I said the very same thing as soon as we walked through the door," Irene chimes in from behind me. "I'm in love with this apartment. It already feels like home to me."

***

"Two spa certificates and dinner at Axel compliments of the hotel," I tell my assistant. "Tom and Irene Clarkson. I want that set up within the next hour."

I end the call as I watch Maya round the corner from the corridor that leads to the private elevator.

I held back as she said her goodbyes to the Clarksons. I didn't want to crowd her. Her job is to sell this space. Mine is to give her the room to do that.

"Shit," she mumbles under her breath as she comes to an abrupt halt near the kitchen counter. "Goddamn it."

I laugh. "What's the problem?"

She lifts her left foot inches off the floor. "The strap on my shoe came loose again. I keep meaning to drop them off to get fixed, but they're one of my favorite pairs of sandals and I don't want to be without them."

I close the distance between us in measured, heavy steps before I drop to one knee in front of her.

She gasps. "Julian, get up. What are you doing?"

I reach forward to grab her foot. I rest it on my thigh. "I'm having a look at your shoe."

She tries to pull her foot away, but I cup my hand over the back of her calf. "Maya, please."

I feel the shiver that courses through her. "Julian."

My name is a whispered threat. She's warning me. I should heed that, but I don't. Instead, I slide my hand further up the back of her calf. "It will only take me a minute to tighten it, Maya. You need to hold still."

She reaches down to balance herself with a hand on my shoulder. "I'll stay still."

I get to work on the strap, pulling it taut before tucking it under another strap and looping it through. "It'll stay in place."

"Thank you," she says softly. "You can get up now."

I can. I should, but I don't.

Instead, I look up into her sky blue eyes and those lips. The beautiful pink lips that have been tempting me since I first saw them in Falon's studio.

I hold her gaze as my hand begins a slow path back up her leg. Her skirt is short. It's short enough that I could flip it over easily and rest my mouth against the front of her panties. One sharp twist and her panties would be gone and she'd feel my tongue sweeping over her core.

"You're an incredibly beautiful woman, Maya." I inch my hand higher until it settles at the back of her thigh. Her skin is smooth and warm.

"We shouldn't." She stares down at me.

I made her a promise that I wouldn't push her to break that fucking rule about not dating a man who just went through a breakup.

If she only knew how many nights I've fucked my fist since I first met her. I lost track months ago. Coming alone in my shower while thinking about her became more fulfilling than an actual fuck.

I carefully move her leg and stretch back up to my feet. I look down at her. I see the same thing in her eyes that I feel inside of me.

"Thank you for the dance, Maya." I reach forward to glide my lips over her cheek. "It was the highlight of my day."

I stop when I feel her hand reach for my shoulder once again. She takes a deep breath. "Julian."

My name is a plea this time, an unsheltered need for more. "Show me, Maya. Show me that I'm worth breaking your rules for."

She does. Her lips move to mine and when I cup my hand behind her head and seal my mouth over hers, I know that it's a kiss that will change me forever.

Chapter 18

Maya

He holds me in place with a firm hand on the back of my head. It's just as hot as the way he took over the kiss. His lips are soft. His breath sweet and when he slid his tongue over my bottom lip, I invited him inside. His tongue is thick and hot as he lashes it against mine, trying to coax more from me.

His other hand moves to my back, sliding up and down it in a motion meant to soothe me. It does. I melt into his arms like a snowflake against a hot piece of metal.

"God, Maya," he whispers those words into my mouth before he nips at my bottom lip. "You're making me so hard. Christ, I'm hard."

He is. I feel his erection between us, pressing against me. It's thick and swollen.

A part of me wants to fuck him right here, on the kitchen counter. I wiggle against him, wanting him to take more.

He pulls back a touch to look into my eyes. His breathing is as labored as my own. His skin is flush.

"Now, that's what I call a kiss."

The sound of an unfamiliar voice snaps us apart. Julian turns around and I grab for the edge of the counter as I crane my neck to find the source of the interruption.

"Irene," I say her name under my breath as I run my hand along my now swollen bottom lip.

I focus on her and Tom and one of the hotel doormen standing a foot behind her.

"We didn't mean to interrupt." She shakes her head. "I must have dropped my scarf when we were dancing. The sweet doorman brought us back up."

I shake off the arousal that has claimed every inch of my body and soul and I take a step toward the main living area. "I'll help you look for it."

"That kiss reminded me of my first kiss with Tom," she says quietly as she steps in place beside me. "That man adores you, Maya. You're a very lucky girl."

I look back at Julian who is already sliding his suit jacket back on.

"I'm a very lucky man, Irene," he says as he steps forward to pick up her scarf from where it fell next to the sofa.

I smile as I watch him hand it to her. "I have a meeting to get to. It was a pleasure meeting you both. I'll call you later, Maya."

He walks away and I suddenly hope that the promised call will include an invitation to dinner.

***

"Why the frown, sunshine?" Tilly asks as she fills a pot with water and places it on my stove. "I come over to cook dinner for my sister, and she looks like the world is about to end."

She's being overly dramatic, as usual.

I'm disappointed. I was anxious to talk with Julian after I realized that he'd left his silver cufflinks at the penthouse. I thought about going to his office to return them, but when I called his personal cell to ask if he was available it went straight to voicemail.

A quick call to his assistant also went to voicemail and by the time she finally called me back, she told me that Julian had left for the day and asked her not to disturb him unless it was an emergency.

Lost and found cufflinks don't constitute an emergency in my books.

"I was hoping to have dinner with someone else."

She holds the knife in her hand over her chest. "Way to stab me in the heart, Maya. Why don't you go ahead and tell me that you love Frannie more than me? You might as well twist the knife in there while you have the chance."

I laugh. Frannie and Tilly are identical twins. Naturally, I can tell them apart because I've known them forever. They were born a year-and-a-half after I was and being their big sister has always been the highlight of my life.

Frannie's settled into her daily routine in San Francisco with her high school boyfriend who is now her husband. They have two daughters, a beautiful home, and an enviable life.

Tilly is the one who envies it the most. She's always wanted to have a life that mirrors Frannie's. When she couldn't find it back home, she moved to New York to chase the dream.

"I love you exactly the same," I say with a grin. "You know that I do."

"I know you love me this much more." She holds her index finger and thumb apart by an inch. "I won't tell Frannie though."

"What are you cooking?"

"A box of our favorite macaroni and cheese and I bought some fresh bread," she answers quickly. "I'm no chef, Maya. Don't expect big things from this kitchen when I'm in it."

"It is my favorite." I look at the box. "I'm glad you're here."

"You wish you were having dinner with the man who owns those cufflinks." She looks over at where I placed Julian's cufflinks on the counter when I got home. "He has excellent taste in accessories."

He also tastes great, or at least his lips do. That's all I got to sample so far.

"Did you sleep with him? Is that why his cufflinks are here?" She pours the dried macaroni into the pot of boiling water.

"No." I shake my head. Tilly and I tell each other almost everything, but I'm not sharing details about Julian, yet. This is new. It's exciting and that nagging voice in the back of my head telling me to be wary because of his ex is still there. "We kissed. He left those at the penthouse after a showing."

She nods. "Here's hoping that he'll be so grateful to have them back that he'll sweep you into his arms and carry you off into forever."

Chapter 19

Julian

"You saved me a boatload of cash, so the least I can do is buy you a bottle of the finest whiskey." I place the brown paper bag in the middle of his desk.

Griffin Kent inches the top of the bag down with the tip of the pen in his hand. "That's not real whiskey, Julian. It's that cheap ass shit we used to drink in high school."

I laugh as I take a seat on the sofa in his office. "Where's Sebastian? I thought he was meeting us here."

"Where he always is; knee deep in someone else's blood while he tries to solve their murder." He yanks the bottle out of the bag and cracks open the lid. "Do you want a drink?"

"No." I wave my hand in the air. "I don't drink cheap whiskey anymore."

"You're an asshole." He laughs as he takes a sip from the bottle. "Christ. That burns all the way down. We must have been desperate when we were sixteen and thought this was it."

"We were typical sixteen-year-olds." I laugh as I drape my arm over the back of the sofa. "Whiskey, weed and women."

"Whiskey, weed and high school girls," he corrects me. "Women now, speaking of which…"

"Isadora's attorney balked at the agreement I had her sign when we started dating. Thank you for that."

Griffin dips his chin. "You're worth too much to fuck around with a woman without something in place to protect your assets."

I was against the idea at first when Griffin proposed it years ago, but he specializes in family law. He's handled a few high profile divorce cases in this city, so he's always looking ahead. It was his idea to arrange for Isadora to sign an agreement that limited her interest in me financially to any shares of the company I'd eventually gift her with. Surprisingly, she agreed to it.

Although we've never lived together, she feels she deserves more now. She doesn't.

"How are you making out with getting her out of the company?"

Griffin knows that the last few weeks haven't been easy. Isadora is still on leave, but that hasn't stopped her from reaching out to our employees to make it known that she feels forced to stay away.

"I'm working on lining up a new job offer for her." I rest my hand on my knee. "I'll know more in a week or two, but she'll trip over her heels if she's offered this. I doubt like hell she'd even step foot back in the Bishop offices if this works out."

"Tell me more." He taps the tip of the pen against the top of his desk.

"I want the deal in place before I share."

I trust him with my life, but I don't have anything firmly in place, so there's no need to explain the details yet.

He rakes his hand through his brown hair. "I'm in the mood for some pool. You game?"

He stands and slides his suit jacket on.

I rise to my feet. "You're on. Loser buys the winner a bottle of scotch."

"The good stuff." He rounds his desk. "No more nostalgic shit for old times' sake."

"I look forward to winning." I follow him out of his office and into the empty reception area. "You're about to lose your shirt."

***

I let the water from the shower run over my back as I palm my cock. It's purple and angry, swollen from thoughts of Maya.

She's been on my mind all day. The touch of her skin on my hand, the taste of her lips on my mouth. If the Clarksons hadn't interrupted us, I would have dropped back to my knees and ate her right there in the penthouse.

I was aching for more when I left, but work got hold of me. It was after ten before I stopped at Griffin's office and near one a.m. when I finally left the bar.

I didn't notice Maya's voicemail until I got home because I don't check my messages as often as I should in the evening. That changes now. I want to be available to her, whenever she needs me.

I turn off the spray and step out into the cold bathroom.

I towel off quickly and pull on a pair of black boxers before I reach for my phone from the counter.

She'll be dead asleep by now but I thumb out a text anyway.

I'm sorry I missed your call, Maya. I'll be in touch first thing tomorrow.

I press send and then walk through the darkened apartment to my bedroom. I toss the phone on the bed and stare out the window.

I hear the faint chime of an incoming text.

Shouldn't you be asleep?

I smile. She's awake as well. My body stirs with the image of her in bed, naked, with one hand holding her phone, the other fingering herself.

I could ask you the same thing.

Her response isn't immediate but I can see she's typing something. I wait patiently, knowing sleep isn't going to find my tonight. I'm too wound up, too wanting.

I have your cufflinks. You left them at the penthouse.

It's not the response I was hoping for but it's better than silence.

I can drop by your place tomorrow and pick them up.

I press send and sit on the edge of the bed. I rub my cock through my boxers. I'll have to come tonight. I feel the sharp bite of need nipping at my spine.

Or…I can come by your place now and drop them off.

I read the message twice before I type out my address and three simple words: *I'll be waiting.*

Chapter 20

Maya

I have no idea what's gotten into me. I went from standing firm in my resolve to not get involved with Julian because of his recent break up with Isadora, to inviting myself over to his apartment in the middle of the night.

If a woman invites herself over to a man's place is that considered a booty call?

I sit in the back of the taxi as the driver steers through the streets of the city. I didn't even read the address Julian sent to me. I was too busy getting dressed and applying a light coat of pale pink lipstick and a sweep of black mascara.

I'm dressed in jeans and a white blouse under a black trench coat. I didn't put a lot of thought into my outfit because I knew that if I did that, I'd second guess my decision to go see him.

"We're almost there," the cab driver announces from the front seat.

I look out at the row of businesses that line the street. "We are?"

"It's a block up." He gestures forward with his chin. "I'll drop you right in front."

I reach in my clutch for a few bills after I glance at the meter. I fish around for the cufflinks, making sure that they're still in the bottom of my purse. I tossed them in there with my keys and some money before I left my apartment.

"You're sure this is the place?" I look out at a shuttered drugstore. "I don't think this is right."

"Is that him?" He points toward the passenger window. "There's a guy lurking in the dark there. Is that your Prince Charming?"

I almost laugh at the comment. As soon as I got in the back seat of the taxi and showed him the text message from Julian with the address, he likely knew what I was doing.

I peer out and spot Julian standing next to the taxi. "That's him."

I place the money in his outstretched palm and slide across the seat. I still can't believe I'm doing this, but there's no turning back now.

***

His apartment is nothing like I imagined it to be. It's smaller than mine, cozier too. It's a one bedroom that sits above the drugstore. He led me partway down the alley to a side door. We had to climb three flights of stairs until we reached his place.

When he opened the door and I stepped inside, I could sense his life all around me.

The furniture is weathered leather. The coffee table is crafted from dark wood. The galley kitchen is tiny with only enough room for one person. He didn't take me down the hallway, but I see two doors. One must be his bedroom, the other the washroom.

"You're surprised, aren't you?" he asks from behind me as he takes my trench coat. "You expected something different."

I did. I expected a penthouse overlooking the park or a brownstone with five floors. "I'm not sure what I expected."

"I bought this place when I was in college." He places my coat on the back of a chair. "I never got around to moving."

"Why move if it feels like home?" I turn to face him. "This feels like a home to me. Your home, I mean."

A smile spreads across his face. "It feels like home to me. It's always felt like home."

I move toward the couch knowing that I need to sit. My knees have been shaking ever since I sent that text message inviting myself over. "I bought an apartment last year that is starting to feel like home."

It is. I've painted it twice with Tilly's help. First, I covered every wall in a light shade of blue and then a month later, I opted for a medium gray. It's still not perfect, but I'm inching closer to it.

"Where do you live?"

"Murray Hill," I answer quickly. "It was a great deal and it's central. I can walk to work. That's important to me."

I open my clutch and reach in. "I should give you back the cufflinks before I forget."

"Tell me why you came, Maya." He takes a seat next to me as he takes the cufflinks and places them on the coffee table.

He's only wearing black sweatpants and a blue T-shirt. I noticed the black ink peeking out from beneath the arm of his shirt almost immediately. I can't tell what it is, but I'm almost as surprised by the tattoo on his bicep as I am his apartment.

"You have a tattoo." I ignore his question. I'm not ready to tell him that I came here to kiss him again. I can't confess that I want more.

"As do you." He reaches for my left hand and tugs it into his lap.

I watch silently as he flips my arm over and carefully unfastens the leather band of the watch I'm wearing. "I saw this at the restaurant the night you were with the Wartons. I've been dying to know what it says."

I don't move as he slides the watch off. He traces his fingertips over the curves of ink on my inner wrist. He does it once and then again before he finally looks at my face. "Enough."

"Enough," I repeat back. "A reminder that I'm enough."

He draws in a quick breath before he brings my wrist to his lips to kiss my skin. "You're so much more than enough. You're everything."

I close my eyes. I don't want to get emotional tonight. I didn't come here to feel anything other than physical pleasure. "Can I see your tattoo?"

He kisses my wrist again before he reaches over his head to tug his T-shirt off.

Jesus. Wow.

Muscles for days, a light smattering of hair on his chest and abs that I could lick all night.

He turns slightly to give me the full view of his left arm. I study the intricate lines of black ink that seamlessly flow together. It's a beautiful piece of art that wraps around his bicep. The word loyalty is at its center.

"Loyalty." I reach up to touch his arm. "It's important to you."

"I value it almost more than I value anything else."

I sigh as I drop my hand. "I never pictured you with a tattoo."

"How did you picture me?"

My brows peak. "What do you mean?"

"You've thought about me, Maya." He turns so he's facing me directly. "Tell me what you've thought about."

I try to slow my heartbeat, but it's useless. I'm the one who decided to come to his place. He knows exactly why I'm here. "Kissing you, touching you."

"We've kissed." He leans forward to kiss me softly. "Was it how you thought it would be?"

"Better." I breathe in his scent as he kisses me again. "It's so much better."

"Show me how you've thought about touching me."

"Now?"

He reaches for my hand. "Touch me, Maya."

I do. I slide my hand from his. I reach for his shoulder first, gliding my fingertips along the cut curves before I move slowly to touch his chest.

He keeps this breathtaking body hidden under his tailored shirts and suits. I knew every inch of him would be incredible.

"I'm aching for you." He slides my hand over the front of his sweatpants, so it's resting on his swollen cock. "I'm taking you to my bed, Maya. Remember what I said about no sleep?"

I nod as he stands and when he holds his hand out to me, I take it. I want this. I want this man more than I've wanted anything in my life.

Chapter 21

Maya

"I've waited so long for this." Julian unbuttons each button on my blouse with languid precision. "I can't tell you how many times I've thought about doing this."

"Taking forever to undress me?" I smile up at him. "I'm not delicate and this isn't an expensive shirt. I'm not against you ripping it off me."

He laughs, throwing his head back. "I want to remember this moment forever. The first time I see your breasts, your pussy. The first taste, the first fuck. I want every detail etched in my mind."

The words are enough to make my knees buckle, but I hold firm to his biceps as he continues his painfully slow unveiling of my body. "Do you remember the first time you saw me?"

That stops his hands in midair. "Your hair was shorter. You were wearing a yellow dress and red heels. I walked into Falon's studio and saw the most beautiful woman in the world."

I remember the dress. I still have it. The heels were tossed out months ago. I can't believe that he can recall all of that. "You have an incredible memory."

"Ask me what I had for dinner two nights ago."

I chuckle. "What did you have for dinner two nights ago, Julian?"

"I have no fucking clue." He winks. "I only remember important things. That's why I remember every time I've ever seen you."

His fingers get to work again and when he finally unbuttons the last button, he slides the thin material from my shoulders to reveal my white lace bra.

I look down at the bed, desperate to be with him. "Can we sit on the bed?"

"Soon." He lowers his mouth to the front of my bra. His breath courses over my skin before he takes my left nipple between his teeth through the lace.

I moan aloud, unable to contain the desperate need I feel. "Take off my bra."

He does. He reaches behind me with one hand and deftly undoes the clasp. The cool air in his bedroom hits me instantly. My nipples were already hard from anticipation and his touch and now they're aching.

"Christ, look at these." He slides my bra off before he tosses it on the floor. "Your nipples are perfect."

He takes my right nipple into his mouth and sucks. I feel his tongue lash against the tender nub.

"I'm close," I whisper with a laugh. "I'm so wet already."

That drops him to his knees. His fingers open the button fly of my jeans to reveal a hint of the white lace G-string underneath.

In one swift movement, the jeans are pooled around my ankles. I step out as he helps me.

"You are wet." His voice is low and thick with desire. "You have an incredible ass. I've wanted my hands on this for years.

Years. He's wanted me for years. As long as I've wanted him.

He kneads the flesh of my bare ass, his head resting against my stomach. I can hear his breathing. It matches my own. Heavy, uneven breaths punctuated with deep sighs.

"I want to make you feel everything, Maya."

I do. I feel more than I ever have before and he's barely touched me.

He moves to slide the lace G-string down. His eyes locked onto the bare skin underneath. "This feels like a fucking dream. Tell me I'm not dreaming this."

I tug on his shoulder to bring him to his feet. "This isn't a dream. It's real."

I want to feel his mouth on me and his fingers inside my core. I want it all but right now, I need my hands on him.

He leans forward to kiss me again and this time it's fevered and deep. He parts my lips instantly with his tongue. He searches for mine before he nibbles at my lips. Small kisses down my neck follow and when I slide my hand under his sweatpants and touch the smooth crown of his cock, he groans.

"A condom." He steps back. "I'm getting a condom."

I touch myself as I watch him undress. The moment I see his beautiful cock, I slide a finger inside me. I chase my own orgasm as I watch him sheath himself and when he pushes me against the wall and wraps my legs around his waist, I come the instant he's inside me.

Chapter 22

Julian

The buzz of my phone wakes me. I turn toward it and that's when I realize that she's here. Maya is in my bed, wrapped around me. Her lush tits are pressed against my side; her leg slung over mine.

I fucked her twice. Once against the wall. The second time on the floor like a man possessed by need.

She screamed my name as she climaxed both times and I swear I'll never hear a sweeter sound than that.

"Your phone," she mumbles under her breath. "You should answer it."

I glance at the clock near my bed. Five a.m. It has to be Paris. My contact there hasn't been able to grasp what a time zone is. I reach over her to grab the phone from where I tossed it on the nightstand after I got up to get her a glass of water.

I don't bother to look at the screen before I answer the call.

"This is Julian."

"I'm coming back to New York. I'm coming back to take back what's mine." Isadora's voice is loud and angry. Too fucking loud for me to shield it from Maya. I know she hears it because she rolls over onto her back and opens one eye.

"I'm hanging up."

"Go ahead." I hear the jingling of keys in the background. "You have some of my things, Julian. I want them back."

That's bullshit. She never left anything here because she loathed this place. Every time she set foot in my apartment, she'd bitch about the size of it. She hated the neighborhood, the furniture, the simple way I've chosen to live.

"Stay away," I say brusquely before I end the call.

Maya's already on her feet next to the bed before I have a chance to stop her. "I'm freaking out right now. I want to run, but I won't."

I watch her rub that tattoo on her wrist. She's naked and beautiful. The soft light that's filtering in from the street illuminates her skin.

"I don't care about her." I pat the bed next to me. "I haven't for a very long time, Maya."

"You broke up just a few weeks ago." She bounces in place. "What if things change? I know we've only spend one night together and our first kiss was yesterday, but I feel things. Not like love things, but really strong like things."

I can't hide my smile. "I feel really strong like things too."

"If you didn't care for her for so long, why stay with her?"

I move to stand too. I want to be on level ground with her. "It was easy to stay with her. Our relationship was primarily about the business. It was uncomplicated."

"Do you like uncomplicated things?"

"No," I answer honestly. "I like things that challenge me. I want someone who makes me feel things I've never felt before. I've felt more alive these past few weeks than I've ever felt before."

"I'm scared, Julian." She sits on the edge of the bed. "I'm so fucking scared that I'll start to feel even stronger things for you and you'll tell me you want her, and not me."

I start to open my mouth to assure her that won't happen, but she stops me with a hand in the air.

"I have to finish. Please let me say my peace."

I nod as I move to sit next to her. "Tell me how you feel."

She slides closer until our outer thighs touch. "I've been hesitant to get serious with anyone for years because of what happened back in San Francisco."

I nod. "I understand."

"I'm not saying this will get serious, but I know that I like being around you and I loved what we just did."

"I loved it more," I crack.

That brings a smile to her full lips. "We'll go again soon and compare notes."

I laugh aloud. I could spend every minute with her. I want to.

"Promise me something." She reaches for both of my hands to cup them in hers.

"Anything," I say as I bring her hands to my lips. "I'll promise you anything."

She leans forward to rest her forehead against mine. "If you start feeling anything for her again, you'll tell me. The second it happens, you'll sit me down and tell me."

"That will never happen, Maya. Never. I don't want anyone but you."

"Promise me," she insists. "Just promise me."

I tug her beautiful bare body into my lap. "I promise."

I hold her until she relaxes in my arms and then I lay her down, slide between her thighs and tongue her to the edge once and then again before I take her clit between my teeth and suck it until she comes.

Chapter 23

Maya

"If your client has an interest in seeing the property for himself, I can arrange that at a time that's most convenient for him."

Todd, the man who arrived for a private showing an hour ago, turns to look at me. He's been standing in the dining area for more than ten minutes, pecking away at his phone.

When he emailed me early this morning to arrange a showing, I was still in bed with Julian. He explained in his message that he's a representative of a buyer who wishes to remain anonymous. It's not uncommon when a property of this value is up for sale.

Many wealthy people want to keep their names and faces out of the financial papers. There's an inherent understanding at Carvel that when this penthouse sells, we'll be screaming about it from the rooftops.

I glance down at my watch. I have another showing in an hour. That one is at Charles Warton Sr.'s apartment. I've been actively promoting that property on my social media pages along with this one.

Interest in the Warton property hasn't been as high but the woman meeting me today is excited. I have a good feeling about her and I don't want to keep her waiting.

"He might actually want to see this place." He holds his phone in the air. "I've been texting pictures to him and he's impressed."

I hope he's impressed enough to make an offer. My time is running out to sell this place before it's handed over to another broker. I need the deal which is why I have Jen calling every person who has viewed the penthouse to get a sense of their interest in it.

"Do you want to set up a time for that showing now?" I tug my cell out of my pants pocket.

I didn't have a lot of time to get ready for work. There was a broker's meeting at the office at nine a.m. so after I left Julian's place, I'd raced home to shower and threw on a pair of navy slacks and a light blue sweater. It's not my idea of the picture perfect business attire, but it's sufficient in a pinch.

"Let me give him a call and I'll find out."

I walk away because I know this man values his privacy. I haven't been able to place whether he's a lawyer or just an assistant hired to handle the initial viewings of properties his boss is interested in.

I take advantage of the time to sneak a peek at my messages. I scroll through them until I spot one from Julian.

You threw the rule book out last night so let's go on an official date. Pizza at seven?

I smile as I read the words. I start to type out a response telling him that I'll meet him anywhere for pizza.

"My client has a window from seven to seven-thirty tonight. Does that work?" Todd asks from where he's standing across the room.

I lower my phone and flash him a genuine smile. "Seven tonight is perfect."

***

"What do I owe you?" I hold my hand on my hip as I turn to the side so he can get a good glimpse of my ass in the tight skirt I'm wearing. "Or do you accept sexual favors in exchange for pizza?"

"Are you offering to blow me to pay your pizza debt?" Julian breezes past me to put the pizza box on the massive island in the penthouse's kitchen. "If you are, forget that damn pizza and get on your knees."

I do. I kick off my heels and drop to my knees in the middle of the penthouse.

My mystery client, a middle-aged man named Simon, left ten minutes ago. I called Julian to tell him I could meet him for pizza but he suggested I stay put. Now, I see why. He wanted to surprise me with a pie and the sight of him in jeans and a hoodie.

I tug down the zipper of his jeans and yank them and his boxer briefs down around his upper thighs.

His cock is hard as stone, curved up to his belly as I run my hands over the length.

"This is better than any pizza I've ever had." I smile as I look up at him. "I've been thinking about doing this since I saw you last night."

He wraps my hair around his fist and pushes my mouth closer to his cock. "I've been thinking about this forever and if you don't suck it now, I'll blow my load all over your beautiful face."

I'd like that. I'd actually love that, but I want to taste him.

I lick the crown with gentle, short sweeps of my tongue. I can tell it's driving him mad with need. His hand tightens in my hair. "In your mouth, Maya."

I slide my mouth over him, gingerly taking as much as I can before I pull back. I repeat it, again and again, stroking the length of his dick with my fist as I suck in more and more of him with each bob of my head.

"You know how to suck cock."

I do. I take him down my throat, swallowing the length of him until he shudders and grabs my head with his other hand.

"Fuck, that's good. Right like that. Like that, Maya."

I give him more of what he wants, taking my time, savoring each sound he makes; every twitch of his cock in my mouth.

He pumps into me, his hips catching an uneven rhythm as he tries to stay steady on his feet.

"I have to come down your throat. Fuck, please let me come down your throat."

I inch closer on my knees. It's a silent sign that I want exactly what he does and when I feel him tense and his heavy balls draw up, I look up and into his face as I swallow every drop of his release.

Chapter 24

Julian

I watch her eat pizza like it's a movie I've been dying to see. She smiles at me with each bite she takes, her eyes closing softly as she chews the food before she swallows.

I wanted the taste of my release to linger on her tongue.

She'd licked me clean after she swallowed my load. Her soft tongue had swept over my entire cock from the base to the tip while she held it carefully in her hand.

I finally pulled her to her feet so I could kiss her. I excused myself to use the washroom, but it was only so I could splash cold water on my face and find my bearings.

I've never been sucked off that way. It was intense, tender, and the most erotic thing I've ever witnessed.

She wasn't in a rush. She didn't pull back when I tugged her closer. She wanted to taste me as desperately as I wanted to taste her last night.

"Did you wear that outfit for your client or for me?"

She looks down at the sheer black blouse she's paired with a black skirt. She's wearing a black bra underneath. It's visible and the thought of another man seeing it makes my stomach clench.

She gestures toward a chair in the dining room. "I had that blazer on and buttoned up when my client was here. I didn't flash him any tits or ass. I'm not that desperate yet. Give it another week and I may start to have nude showings."

Give it a week and this place will be sold. Interest has been high. I know that from speaking to the doorman. A steady stream of potential buyers has been streaming through here. Some are accompanied by a sales agent, but many come to meet Maya. If she can sell this place on her own, the commission is all hers.

"There's a clause in your contract that says no nude showings." I take one last bite of pizza.

"I checked." She wipes her mouth with a paper napkin. "There's not a clause."

I pick up her used napkin and use it to wipe my lips. "Let's talk business for a second."

"I thought we were." She cocks her head. "I told you early on that I'll get this place sold. I want the other eleven units. If it means I have to flash a tit I'll do it."

She's teasing, but it eats at my nerves. "Don't joke about that. I don't want another man to see you nude. I want you for myself."

She chews on her bottom lip but doesn't say a word.

"Don't date anyone else, Maya. Don't fuck anyone else. Agree to be exclusive with me."

She runs her hand through her hair. I see the hesitation in her expression. I know that she's about to bring up the fact that I just left a long-term relationship less than a month ago, but that's bullshit.

I was gasping for air before I met her, now I feel like my lungs are finally full.

I stop her at the pass as she opens her mouth. "Don't talk about her, Maya. I don't know how to make you understand that I was living in a vacuum of emptiness before I saw you at the launch party."

"I was going to say that I'll be your girlfriend." She rounds the island to stand next to me. "I don't want anyone else, Julian. I want it to be just the two of us."

"You'll keep your clothes on when you show the penthouse?" I cock a brow.

"Is that part of the promise because I don't know if I can agree to that?"

I slide my hand over the curve of her ass. "You agree to it. You want it just as much as I do."

"I want you." She turns to face me. "I just want you."

"You have me." I tap my chest with my hand. "I'm yours. Do whatever you want to me, Maya. I mean that."

"I'm going to take you up on that offer." She picks up the pizza box. "Let's trash this and head out. I've seen enough of this penthouse for one day."

***

"So you have two twin sisters?"

Maya laughs as she swings her legs into my lap. We're at my place. We took the subway here after we disposed of the pizza box and left the hotel.

"I have twin sisters. It's kind of implied that there are two of them." She scrolls through the images on her phone. "This is Tilly."

I catch a glimpse of an attractive brunette with a smile like Maya's.

She turns the phone back around so it's facing her. "This is Frannie."

She shows me another image, but the woman looks identical to the one in the other image. "How do you tell them apart?"

"They look different to me. Tilly's nose is a tiny bit smaller. One of Frannie's bottom teeth has a chip in it."

"What was it like growing up with twin sisters?" I run my fingertip over the smooth skin of her leg.

"Wonderful. Horrible."

"Wonderful how?"

Her eyes sweep over my face. I can't tell if she's comfortable talking about this or not. I'm not pushing. It's general curiosity that is feeding this conversation.

"I can call them if I ever need someone to talk to and they'll both drop everything to be there for me. I know they have my back regardless of what's going on. I love that about them."

I have the same dynamic in my relationship with Brynn. We may not see each other that often anymore now that her work on the hotel is complete, but she's a phone call away if I ever need her. That's a type of reassurance that is hard to come by in this world.

"Tell me why it's horrible, Maya."

She purses her lips together. "That might have been the wrong word. It's not exactly horrible, but when you have younger sisters who are adorable, you fade into the background."

I glance down at her arm and the tattoo that is once again hidden beneath the band of a watch. "Is that why you didn't feel like you were enough?"

She hangs her head. "That's part of it. After the twins came I was the helper. I was always the helper and they were always the center of attention. I wouldn't trade any of it, but once I had the chance to venture out and do my own thing, I finally figured out who I was."

"A beautiful woman who is going to claim a spot as one of the top brokers in Manhattan?"

Her smile lights her entire face. "It's something like that. I like taking care of me now. Buying my own place and making decisions about my business. It feels good to put myself first. I like it."

To anyone else it may sound selfish or self-centered, but that's not how I take it. Maya's bold and unapologetic. She wants to succeed in a business that is tough as nails. She's doing it, with grace and kindness.

"I admire you, Maya."

"You admire me?" She wraps her arms around my neck. "You'll need to explain that to me, Julian."

"You followed your own path. You didn't feel the pressure of a family business bearing down on you."

"What do you think you would have been if you weren't an hotelier?" She kisses my chin. "A male model? An exotic dancer?"

I pinch her side. "Jesus, no."

"What then?" She tilts my chin up with her hand now so we're staring into each other's eyes. "If your grandfather hadn't handed you the keys to the Bishop Hotel Empire where would you be working today?"

I've never given it any thought. I knew the path my life had to take when I was a child. It's why I went to college to study business. "I don't know."

Sadness settles over her expression. "Are you happy? Do you like what you do?"

"I love it," I answer quickly. "I'm good at it and it led me straight to you."

She nuzzles her head next to mine as she blows out a soft sigh. "You're one of my favorite people, Julian Bishop."

"You're one of mine, Maya."

Chapter 25

Maya

"Maya?" I hear a man's voice to my left, but when I turn in that direction, I'm greeted with a throng of people all waiting to cross Fifth Avenue.

I shake off the interruption as a mirage and continue walking and typing on my phone even though I know it's hazardous to my health.

"Maya, wait." The voice is louder and closer this time, so I pocket my phone, saving the draft of the note I was working on to remind myself of everything I have to do today, including the most important task.

Irene and Tom Clarkson want another look at the penthouse when they come to town next week so as soon as I'm done with my morning showing at the Warton place, I'm going to give them a call to schedule that.

I turn when I hear the man call my name again. "Jason? Is that you?"

Technically, it's Dr. Jason Hunt.

We dated more than a year ago. It was fun, he was interesting until we both realized that the only thing we had in common was sex.

Fascinating discussions were never part of our dynamic. We'd eat take-out at my place, head to my bed and he'd be out the door within minutes after finishing.

"You look incredible." He pulls me into a tight embrace. "It's been months since I've seen you."

"How are you?" I step back and look at his face. He's handsome. I always thought that. His face isn't sculpted like Julian's, but he's definitely attractive.

"Good. I'm good." He shoves his hands into the front pockets of his jeans. "I've been meaning to call you."

I smile. I know where this is headed. We hooked up twice after the end of our relationship. It was within weeks of our breakup and it only prolonged the inevitable. The next time he hit me up for a quickie, I shut him down. I haven't heard a word since.

"About?" I raise a brow.

"I'm on the market for a new place."

I squeeze my eyes shut. "I don't handle rentals anymore, Jason."

"You're a full-fledged broker now."

I look at him again. "You know that?"

"I take a peek at your profile on the Carvel website from time-to-time," he admits. "I like your hair like that."

It's the same as it was when we were sleeping together. It's just longer now. I, on the other hand, am wiser.

"Thank you. So you're looking to buy?"

He nods. "Exactly. I want to invest in a decent property. It's time to throw my money into a mortgage instead of rent."

"I'm swamped right now, but I can set you up with another broker from my firm if that works for you."

I can tell by the obvious disappointment on his face that it's not the answer he was expecting. "When will you have time to show me a few places? I trust your judgment, Maya, and besides, you know what I like."

The inference is there in his words. He's not talking about white cabinetry and oak floors. "I'm in a relationship."

"Is it serious?"

That's none of his business, but I answer anyway. "I'm not sure, yet. It's new. It's early."

"If that changes, call me." He lets out a sigh. "It would be good to catch up."

I don't respond because I have no idea what to say. As much fun as I had in the past with Jason, it doesn't compare to what I have with Julian now. I won't risk that by taking on an ex as a client. There are plenty of brokers in this city who would be more than willing to help Jason find a place to call home. I just don't happen to be one of them.

***

I finish my workday with a coffee meeting with Jen and then a call to Julian. He doesn't answer. I try his assistant who once again tells me that Julian is unavailable unless it's an emergency.

My desire to sit in his lap and ride his cock isn't really a life or death situation even if I'm desperate to come.

128

I decide to invite my sister out for dinner. Our time together has been limited as of late. With all the hours I'm putting in trying to sell the Warton residence and the Bishop Hotel penthouse, I feel like I've lost my grip on my life.

Falon is in Memphis this week with Asher while he works with a new group of musicians on a song he just wrote. I made a note in my calendar to touch base with her before the week is out so I can see her once she's landed back in New York.

"Where do you want to go for dinner, Tilly?" I ask as soon as she picks up my call. "Name the place. It's my treat."

"I have a blind date."

"Why is this the first time I'm hearing about it?"

She laughs. It's light and filled with joy. "Maybe because you've been ignoring me for weeks now. I've had to risk life and limb to meet strange men on my own."

"That ends tonight. I'll spy on you like the good old days."

I hear movement. "I'm just about to walk out the door. I'm meeting him at a bar on the corner of Forty-Second and Third in twenty minutes."

"You need to haul ass if you're going to make it there in time," I point out. Since I'm less than three blocks from there, I start walking in that direction. "I'll see you there, but ignore me unless he's a jerk."

"Thanks for having my back, Maya. I've missed you."

I bite back a tear. "I've missed you too, Tilly."

Chapter 26

Maya

"You didn't even bother to sit down?" I motion to the bar stool next to me. "Sit here and tell me what was wrong with him."

Tilly slips onto the stool next to me. "There wasn't anything wrong with him, but he definitely wasn't the same age as the guy in the picture I saw online."

That's one of the reasons why I've never been into meeting men online. I've heard Tilly tell me over and over about how many men don't use an actual picture of themselves, or if they do, the image is decades old. She unwittingly ended up having dinner with a seventy-year-old man a few months ago.

She had a good time but not in the traditional sense of a date. It was more a granddaughter, grandfather connection.

"Let's talk about you." She takes a sip of my martini. "Do you do anything other than work? Did you ever see the cufflink guy again?"

I start with work because that's easy. "This month is the most amazing I've ever had in my career. I'm close to selling an apartment on Central Park West and if I can sell that penthouse at the Bishop Hotel, I'll have the opportunity to sell eleven more suites there. The commission alone is enough to pay off my mortgage, Tilly."

"Seriously?"

"It's ridiculous." I chuckle. "I'm selling properties that I'll never be able to afford, yet it feels completely natural to do it."

"Do you have any interested buyers in the Bishop Hotel place?"

I sip on my drink. "There's this sweet older couple. They're moving to New York to be closer to their son and his family. They loved the place. They're coming back to Manhattan before the month is over so I'll show it to them again."

"That's a great sign, isn't it?"

It is. It's promising. I've had clients who've looked at properties once and have made an offer. Others have toured apartments more than a dozen times before declaring that it's not for them. I'm hoping Tom and Irene will fall even more in love with the penthouse the next time they see it.

"I'm crossing my fingers that it'll work out with them."

She finishes my drink in one swallow. "This is good. We should order two more."

I hold up two fingers to the bartender. He nods.

"What about the cufflink guy? Did that amount to anything?"

I'm hesitant to talk about Julian because I know how much Tilly wants to find someone to share her time with. She's not the jealous type, but seeing Frannie happily married with children, eats at Tilly in a way I don't fully understand. I can't empathize because I'm not at the stage where marriage or children fits into my life.

"Spill the beans, Maya. I want to know."

I pick up a pretzel from a bowl on the bar and pop it into my mouth. I take that few seconds to consider exactly how to phrase what I'm about to say.

"Did you sleep with him?" she asks with a glint in her eye. "I don't want details, but is it like that? Are you involved?"

I nod. "We kissed and then spent most of that night together. Things have happened since then too."

"Maya." She grabs hold of my forearm. "It sounds serious. Is it or is it more a fuck buddy thing?"

I feel a rush of relief when the bartender sets our martinis down in front of us. I gulp half of mine in one swallow. "He's not a fuck buddy type, Tilly. We're exclusive. We decided to date just each other."

"You have a boyfriend?" She lifts the glass to her lips before she sets it down without taking a drink. "What's he like? Tell me his name."

It's inevitable. I can't hide this from her. I don't want to even though I know she's going to put two-and-two together.

"I'm dating Julian Bishop, Tilly."

"You're not." Her mouth falls open before she slams it shut. "You're dating a client?"

"He's an amazing man. He's so different than anyone I've ever known." I feel my face flush. "Everything about him is perfect."

She stops me with a hand on my shoulder. "He's not perfect, Maya. Don't go into this expecting him to be perfect. He'll disappoint you."

She's right, of course. There isn't a perfect person walking the face of this earth, but Julian comes damn close. "I know that, Tilly. I meant he's good for me. He treats me right."

"He better." She waves her closed fist in the air. "If he hurts you, he's going to have to deal with me."

"He won't hurt me, "I say it even though a part of me is still scared that he will. "I pray he won't ever hurt me."

***

"I'm taking the subway. Do you want to come with me?" Tilly wraps her coat tighter around her. "Where the hell did this wind come from?"

"You have Mother Nature to thank for that." I glance down the street. "I'm going to walk for a bit and then I think I'll catch a taxi."

"Suit yourself." She pulls me close to her. "I love you, Maya. I'm happy for you. You're getting everything you deserve."

I want the same for her. I know that she loves her work and her friends, but I see the sadness in her eyes. Tilly has so much to give, and one day, a man is going to walk into her life and see that. Hopefully, it will be a man who isn't trying to pass off a picture of someone else as his own.

"I love you too." I squeeze her tightly. "Text me when you get home, so I know you're safe."

"If you'd let me live with you, I'd always be safe."

I hold up my phone. "Text me, Till."

She nods before she darts down the street toward the subway.

I start the walk down Third Avenue. Since I've moved to New York, I've become accustomed to the unique nuances of every neighborhood. It was an important part of the learning curve for my job. It's near impossible to help anyone find a property if you don't know the type of community they crave.

I stop to look in the darkened windows of shops and I read the posted menus on the windows outside two restaurants.

It's when I reach the third that I stop and stare inside.

I'll never get over how handsome he is. Julian is sitting at a small table with two other men. They each have a bottle of beer in front of them and a plate of food. They're dressed casually and it's easy to see that it's not a business meeting.

These must be his friends. This is a part of his life I want in on.

He looks happy and all I want to do is stand here all night and soak in that smile, but I bundle my coat around me and take off so I can go home and dream about him.

Chapter 27

Julian

"Do you have a minute or two?"

I look up to see Maya standing in the doorway to my office.

I wasn't expecting to see her. I'd spent last night with Griffin and Sebastian eating Greek food and talking about our days playing high school football.

I was tempted to call Maya on my way to the subway after dinner, but I didn't. She'd left me a voicemail telling me that she was going to spend time with her sister, so I didn't want to interrupt that.

She takes a step forward before I can scramble to my feet. I push back from the desk and round it quickly. "I didn't expect to see you here."

She looks back into the common area outside my office where a few employees are gathered with laptops.

I brush past her to close the door. "Do you want anything? Coffee? Water?"

She shakes her head. "I'm fine. I'm good. I can't stay long. I'm meeting Charles Warton in a few minutes."

I take a step closer and tug her into my arms. She's dressed as stylishly as always in a blue dress and nude heels. She takes care in presenting herself to her clients in a soft and approachable way. It's just another reason why I'm so insanely attracted to her.

"Did you have fun with your sister?"

"I did. Her blind date was a bust, but we hung out for a bit. I told her about you."

I step back so I can look at her face. "You told her about me?"

"Not every detail." Her eyebrows dance. "I mentioned I was seeing someone and that his name happens to be Julian Bishop."

I feel something I can't place. Maybe it's pride or excitement, but I like that her sister knows that we're together. I want more people to know but that time will come after I've closed the last chapter of my life. "I'd love to meet her sometime."

The corner of her mouth curves into a small smile. "I'd like that too."

"Maybe the three of us can grab a bite sometime?" I don't push to make plans now because I want Maya to set the pace for this. I'm more than happy to spend every second we do have together alone, but I won't pass the opportunity to get to know someone who is important to her.

"We can make that happen." Her eyes drop to her hand when her phone chimes. She swipes her finger across the screen before she lets out a deep sigh.

"Is something wrong?" I study her face, watching her brow knit.

She makes a frustrated noise. "I saw a man I used to date yesterday. Jason. This is him texting me now."

Irritation simmers inside of me. I know who he is. Jason Hunt, a doctor. He was with Maya for months before they ended their relationship. "Where did you see Jason?"

She shifts her feet. "On the street. He's looking for an apartment. He asked if I could help him find a place to live."

I trust her. I know that she's not the type of woman to fuck one man and then crawl into another's bed the same day. "Are you considering taking him on as a client?"

"It would be awkward. I suggested he talk to another broker from Carvel, but he said he wants to wait to see if I become available to help him."

"If you become available to help him?" I arch a brow.

"I told him I was involved with someone. I didn't want him to have any false hope."

I'm relieved. I'm also annoyed that he's confident that she'll be available at some point to help him find a place to live or a place to fuck her. "It sounds like you took the best approach with him."

"Have you told Isadora about us?" She pushes her phone into her purse.

"No," I answer truthfully. "I see no reason to bring your name into what's going on between us."

"What is going on between you?"

I see confusion written all over her face. I want to soothe her and chase it away, but that's impossible. Isadora called earlier demanding a meeting. My assistant directed her to Chloe, but she's insistent on speaking to me directly.

I'm days away from securing Isadora a new job, but until that happens, I have to keep her at bay.

I rake both hands through my hair. "I'm leaving it all to my attorney. She's handling Isadora."

It's not enough of an answer to satisfy her but her time is limited. I can tell when she glances at the clock hanging on my wall. "I need to meet Charles."

"Can I see you tonight?"

She chews on the corner of her lip. I already know that's a sign of agitation for her. "Can we figure that out later? I have a full day. I'm not sure when it will be over."

I'm disappointed, naturally, but I won't push for more than she wants to give me. "I'll be thinking about you, Maya. I always do."

The corners of her mouth curve into a soft smile. "With or without my clothes on?"

"You're determined to leave me with a hard-on." I curve my arm around her back to press her body to mine. "I'll have to go fuck my fist if I want to get any work done today."

"I think I just came." She kisses me softly. "I want to watch you do that."

"As long as I get to watch your fingers slide over your tight little pussy."

She inches even closer. "I like you, Julian."

"I like you too, Maya." I kiss her one last time before she leaves me, and my aching cock, behind.

***

Being a ruthless son-of-a-bitch is a requirement if you want to get ahead in this town. That is one of the most common misconceptions out there.

A man, or a woman, can be an honest, hard-working soul and they'll work their way to the top, right next to those who step on others on their way up.

I've never considered myself an asshole, but there are certain people who bring out the bastard in me. The man sitting in my office now is one of them.

"The deal I worked out is with Isadora." Bruce Tortin runs his finger along the edge of my desk. "I want her in this meeting. I won't negotiate with you, Julian. You can go to hell."

I want something he has and I need to find a way to get that without involving Isadora. "Bruce, Isadora is on leave. I have a highly qualified legal staff. You can pick any of them to come to the meeting if you feel the need to have my counsel present."

He should have his lawyer here, but Bruce doesn't waste money on essentials like an attorney skilled in the art of negotiation. He's been working strictly with Isadora to hammer out a deal to sell Bishop the four boutique hotels he owns in California.

All four of them are currently running with a loss. I have every intention of changing that.

My plan is simple. I'll purchase them, rebrand them as Bishop Properties and redesign them. I just need his signature on the dotted line.

"Get Isadora in here now or the deal is off."

I need the deal on. I've already purchased six other hotels in the state that I'll rebrand and launch at the same time. If I don't secure Bruce's hotels, it puts the entire investment we've already made in jeopardy.

"You're being unreasonable, Bruce."

He moves to stand. "Get her down here, Julian, or I walk."

Chapter 28

Maya

I gasp when Anne pops the lid off the bottle of champagne in her hands. "You officially sold the Warton apartment, Maya. Congratulations!"

I'm ecstatic. Charles was thrilled with the offer I presented him with, and the buyer is eager to move in. The deal will close in thirty days and barring a catastrophe, I'll have my commission check in my hand soon after.

"It's my biggest sale to date." I take the glass of champagne from her hand. "I'm hoping that by the end of this month, we'll be toasting again."

"Faith, Maya." Anne takes a sip of the bubbly. "Have faith and the buyer will come."

The truth is that I'm losing faith. I've put most of my eggs in the Clarksons' basket. They'll be back in New York in four days, and if I can convince them that the Bishop penthouse is the ideal place to dance their nights away, I'll close on that sale soon too.

All of our other leads have dried up.

"What are you going to do to celebrate?" She puts down her glass. "I can't indulge anymore right now. I have a meeting with our junior agents in ten minutes."

I giggle. "You can take the rest of the bottle home to share with your husband after work."

"That I will do unless you want it to share with your special someone."

I have other plans for Julian.

When I visited him at his office earlier today, that was on a whim. I didn't know what to expect, but the flirting was hot. I haven't been able to shake the image of him masturbating from my mind all day, so my plan is simple.

I'll show up at his office again unannounced with a surprise under my trench coat and a smile on my face.

I'm betting that it'll be a day both of us will remember for a very long time.

***

"He's in a meeting." Julian's assistant looks over her shoulder toward his slightly ajar office door. "I'd let you say hi, but it's an important one." I scratch the back of my neck. I feel exposed even though my black silk bra and panties are covered by my coat. The only other thing I'm wearing is a pair of shoes. They're the same strappy heels Julian tried to fix for me. "Is there a place I can wait?"

She gestures to a sofa that is situated a few feet from her desk. The office is set up to be a welcoming space for all employees. They come and go as they please, stopping to chat with his assistant or to park themselves down in one of the chairs or the sofa while they work.

I take a seat even though I'm tempted to ignore what she said in favor of seeking out Julian. I don't because I want him to respect my work and in order to do that, I have to respect his.

I tug my phone from the pocket of my coat and text a quick message to Jen asking if she's been able to reach Simon, the man who viewed the apartment the other night.

She doesn't respond immediately which isn't surprising. I have her working her ass off right now, trying to conjure up more potential buyers.

"Can I get you a coffee?" Julian's assistant asks. "I'm heading down for my break and I can bring you back one."

I sigh. If she's expecting me to still be waiting by the time she's done her coffee break it might be time for me to pack up and head home. "How long do you think Julian will be?"

She shrugs as she pushes back from her desk. "Let's give it ten minutes. I'll come back from my break early and if he's still in there, I'll poke my head in his office and see what I can find out."

I smile. I like her. "That's a deal and I'll take a coffee."

As she heads around the corner, I stand. I tug on the belt of my trench coat to tighten it. The smooth black fabric slides through my palm easily.

I look down at the watch I'm wearing. It says it's seven p.m. I wish it were true. By that time tonight, I'll hopefully be in Julian's arms or in his bed.

"I'll always come when you need me, darling."

I look toward the sound of that voice. It's the unmistakable voice that I listened to during a lecture about women in business. It's the same voice that greeted me at the launch party last month when she thought I was making a move on her boyfriend.

I glance at Julian's office door as she exits with him on her heel. "I'm grateful, Isadora."

"You know how important this is to me, Julian." She turns so her back is to me. "I'd fly to the ends of the earth for you."

I can't see his face because her head is blocking my view, but I can hear every word that he's saying. "I do appreciate it. Thank you."

"So, we'll meet at seven at Normand's?"

"Axel Tribeca," he corrects her.

She inches back on her heels. "I'll see you there."

He doesn't notice me when she turns to make her way toward the elevator. Instead, he walks back into his office, shutting the door behind him.

Chapter 29

Maya

I don't leave because I'm not a coward who runs from something she cares for at the first sign of trouble. I'm also primed to fight. My blood has been simmering with anger ever since Isadora left and Julian shuttered himself away in his office.

I count the minutes until his assistant comes back from her break. It's thirteen, three more than the ten she promised but it's still not enough time to calm me down.

The temptation to walk over and push open the door to his office was strong, but I've always tried to cool down before I confront anyone. Words said in anger are often never forgotten.

"Oh, his door is closed now?" She glances over at it as she hands me a paper cup filled with coffee. "That's a sign that he doesn't want to be disturbed."

I want him to be disturbed. I need him to be disturbed right now.

"Can you tell Julian that Maya is here to see him?"

"You're Maya?" She lowers herself into her chair. "You didn't say you were Maya when you got here."

"Does it matter?"

She nods briskly as she picks up the bulky phone from her desk. "Maya is here. I'm sorry, sir, but she's been waiting for some time now. I didn't know it was her."

I arch a brow as I listen to her rattle on to Julian.

By the time she's placed the receiver of the phone back in its cradle, his office door swings open.

He shuts the door behind him before he closes the distance between us with heavy steps. He no longer has his suit jacket or tie on. The sleeves of his blue dress shirt are rolled up.

"Maya." He stops abruptly when he reaches me. "What is it? Is everything alright?"

I'm tempted to flash him on the spot, but I'm not wasting my expensive lingerie on him after seeing him with Isadora. "I came to surprise you."

"It's not a good time." He glances at his assistant before he looks at me. "I'm in the middle of something right now."

"You asked me when I was here earlier if you could see me tonight. The answer is yes." I thread two of my fingers through the bottom of my hair.

It feels as though my heart is thrumming against the wall of my chest as I wait for him to respond.

"Can you come to my place at ten?" His gaze darts back to his office. It's beginning to make me wonder who else he has hidden in there.

"I'd prefer dinner at seven. I'm celebrating. I'd like to do that with you." It's a bitch move, and I know it. I'm setting a trap. I'm settling in to see if he'll take the bait and then I'll catch him so I can watch him writhe and squirm.

"Celebrating what?"

"I sold the Warton property today," I say proudly even though I'm standing in his office in my underwear holding the weight of the world on my shoulders.

His eyes search mine as a smile glides over his mouth. "That's incredible. That does call for a celebration."

"So we'll have dinner together? It will be our first official date."

His gaze drops to the floor as he swallows. "I have somewhere I need to be at seven. Unfortunately, I can't break those plans."

You can break my heart though. I feel it happening. I won't cry because that gives this void inside of me more space than I want it to have.

"I'll call you when I'm free, Maya. We can celebrate in our own way."

"Mr. Bishop? Sir?" His assistant is back on her feet. "I just received an email that requires your urgent attention."

"Take care of that," I say with a flippant wave of my hand.

He does. He rounds her desk, bends down and reads whatever is displayed on the screen of her computer.

I don't bother waiting for him to finish. I leave with the knowledge that I have a job to do. I have a penthouse to sell, and nothing, not even Julian Bishop and his ex-girlfriend are going to keep me from making that happen.

***

I step into the lobby of the Bishop Hotel Chelsea at ten minutes after seven. I had no plans to go out tonight. After I left Julian's office, I went back to my apartment and promptly fell asleep in the middle of my bed.

It was mid-afternoon, but I felt exhausted and even though I intended to make a quick pit stop there to put on clothes, I decided to soothe my aching bones and within minutes I was out like a light.

My phone ringing woke me up twenty minutes ago. I ignored it at first and wrapped a blanket around me, but when it rang again, and then again, I finally answered.

It was the manager of this hotel. She told me that she needed me down here as soon as possible. I questioned her because my bed was winning the internal battle over whether I wanted to venture out or roll over and stay the night wrapped in its warmth.

All she'd say is that it was an important matter that needed my immediate attention. Curiosity alone got my ass out of bed after that.

I pulled on a black dress, slipped my feet into a pair of heels and headed straight out the door.

"Can you find Lindsay for me?" I ask the clerk at the front desk. "She called me a few minutes ago about the penthouse."

"Are you Maya?" The young man behind the desk offers me a kind smile.

I nod.

"I was told to send you right up." He points toward the private elevator in the corner of the lobby. "You have your key card, right?"

I flash it in the air. "I'm all set. I guess I'll head up."

I make my way across the lobby wondering what the hell was so important that it brought me here on a night when all I want is to be left alone.

***

I hear soft music when the elevator doors open. I step off and into the corridor that leads to the central living space.

"Lindsay?" I call out the hotel manager's name because I was hoping to have a chance to talk to her about what the issue is before I have to face it head-on.

On the way over here, I ran every possible scenario through my mind. This penthouse is secure and it's manned by a state of the art alarm system. If anything had triggered that, someone at Bishop's main offices would have been called, not me.

I'm the listing agent which means that the problem has to be related to that in some capacity.

"Lindsay?" I say her name against as I near the end of the corridor.

My breath catches in my chest when I round the corner and take in the main living space.

The lighting is dim, but I can still clearly see the scene set out in front of me. There's a beautiful setting on the dining room table for two. Three bouquets of flowers make up the centerpieces and several lit candles give the table a romantic ambiance.

A man in a chef's uniform is standing next to the table along with a woman dressed in black slacks and a white dress shirt. She's holding a circular tray with two glasses on it; two glasses of champagne.

It's when she steps to the side that I notice him. He's wearing the same tuxedo he had on the night of this hotel's launch. His hair is neatly pushed back from his face. His jaw is cleanly shaven. He looks every inch the perfect date.

"Julian," I say his name softly. "What's happening?"

"We're celebrating your latest accomplishment, Maya." He approaches with steady steps. "I couldn't pass up the chance to spend the night with you."

Chapter 30

Julian

I take her in my arms not caring that there are others mere feet away watching us. I kiss her tenderly, softly even though I want more. I'll take more, later when we're alone.

"You said you had plans." She looks past me to where the chef and server are standing in wait. "You said they were unbreakable."

When I said that this afternoon I believed it was true. I was in panic mode and frustrated to hell and back that I had to deal with Isadora.

Once Maya stormed out of my office, clarity set in. I'd let her walk away believing that something on this earth was more important than celebrating with her.

"I want to explain all of that to you, Maya." I kiss her again. "I fucked up when you came to see me. I should have told you then that I was dealing with Isadora and the takeover of another hotel. "

Hearing my ex-girlfriend's name stiffens Maya's shoulders. "I have a confession."

I want her to be comfortable, so I unbutton her coat and help her slide it off. She's dressed impeccably in a simple little black dress.

I turn toward the chef and server. "We'll need a few minutes."

They nod in unison and walk toward the kitchen, but not before the server places the tray on the dining room table. I'm paying them both a small fortune so their time tonight belongs to me. If I keep them here until the stroke of midnight, neither will complain.

"Can we sit?" Maya moves toward one of the dining room chairs, but I stop her mid-step to steer her toward the leather sofa that faces the wall of windows.

She lowers herself onto it, and I do the same, taking a seat right next to her. "Confess, Maya."

Her eyes search my face before she reaches up to run a finger over my jaw. "You're beautiful. Do people ever say that to you?"

They do. Years ago, a magazine coined me as the sexiest man alive, twice. I laughed it off at the time. It made me uncomfortable and challenged my view of myself. I know I'm attractive. I hear it often, but with Maya I know she sees deeper within.

"Not as often as people say it to you."

That brings a squeak of laughter from her. "Somehow I doubt that's true."

"I'm excited for you," I say it because it's been something I've wanted to share with her since this afternoon. "Selling the Warton apartment is a big deal. It's a huge step forward for your career."

She kisses me, parting my lips with the tip of her tongue. I moan when her teeth scratch my bottom lip.

"You're making it hard for me not to take you home with me right now, Maya."

As she pulls back, her blue eyes lock on mine. "The second time I came to your office today I was wearing only my panties and bra."

My cock swells instantly. "When we were talking, you were wearing next to nothing under your coat?"

"Just the panties and bra I have on under this dress."

I'm tempted to rip the dress apart to get my eyes on what I missed out on earlier. I was too wrapped up in the potential deal to notice.

Fuck.

"Jesus, Maya." I run my hand over her knee. "You're driving me crazy here."

"I lied to you." She rests her forehead against mine. "Technically, it wasn't a lie, but it feels like a lie to me."

As long as what she feels for me isn't a lie, I can deal with anything else.

"Explain what you mean." I cup her chin in my hand. "What feels like a lie, Maya?"

She lifts her hand to her forehead and rubs. "I saw Isadora at your office. I heard you make plans with her and then I tried to make plans at the same time. I wanted to see which one of us you'd choose."

***

I gulp down both glasses of champagne from the tray before I move to sit next to her again.

Her confession about Isadora took me to my feet. I was angry, embarrassed, frustrated and so aroused that I could have fucked her on the sofa with the chef and server looking on. I wouldn't have cared if all of the city would have seen my driving my dick into her.

"I should have said something." She drags her hands through her hair. "I heard her call you darling. I heard you tell her that you wanted to see her at seven. I was mad, Julian. I was so fucking mad at you."

Christ, I need to fuck her.

"You believed that I was meeting her for what reason, Maya? A date? A prelude to a night together?" I keep my tone neutral.

She shrugs. "I have no idea. I was blind with rage at that moment."

I replay the events of the afternoon in my mind. "Isadora left a good fifteen minutes before we spoke. Were you waiting for me that entire time?"

She nods. "When I first arrived your assistant said you were in an important meeting. I told her I'd wait. She went for a break, and when she came back, that's when I told her to call you."

"She's aware that if you ever need to see me or speak to me, that I'm available," I say under my breath.

She turns to look right at me. "I didn't tell her who I was until she called you."

"I hate games, Maya." I drop my gaze to the floor. "I'm sorry that you had to witness that exchange between Isadora and me, but you were wrong in not confronting me on the spot."

Her bottom lip quivers. "She called you darling. You made plans to see her."

"So you hatched a plan to test me?" I feel my jaw tick.

She folds her arms in front of her. "Yes, and you failed that test."

I shake my head slightly. She's infuriating and I'm still hard as stone. "I'd argue that you can't fail a test that you're not aware you're taking. I didn't have all the facts, Maya."

"You had all the facts you needed to make a choice." She rubs her temples. "It doesn't matter now. You obviously canceled your plans with her to do this for me."

I won't lie to her. I can't. "I saw Isadora an hour ago."

"Where?" she spits the question about between clenched teeth.

I move closer to her but she backs away, her hands flying in the air to ward me off.

"Where did you see her?" she hisses the words out this time.

"In the bar downstairs."

Her gaze floats over my shoulder before she levels her eyes on mine. "Did you bring her up here?" I love the jealousy. It's stirring my need for her even more. I want her this possessive, this willing to fight for me but I know what this is doing to her inside. "You know that I didn't. You know I wouldn't fuck her again. Don't think with your head, Maya. Feel with your heart."

She swallows. "Why didn't you choose me at your office? Why did you choose her?"

"I chose business." I lean back on the sofa. "I had a deal hinging on Isadora's involvement. She had to be there to make it happen. What you saw at my office was an agreement to meet to discuss the acquisition of another hotel chain. The owner of that hotel would only agree to move forward with Isadora on board. He was in my office as well."

"Once I spoke to you and gave it a moment of thought, I knew I had to see you tonight," I go on," I called Isadora and the other hotel chain's owner and met them downstairs to finalize the deal."

"I didn't know."

"You were hurt in the past, Maya, but I'm not him." I exhale harshly. "I'm working very hard to get Isadora out of the business, but until that happens, I need to see her from time-to-time and meet with her."

"I hate her," she says with a laugh.

I lean toward her. "There's nothing personal going on between us anymore. Trust me on that and promise me no more games."

"No more games," she says quietly. "I promise."

Chapter 31

Maya

I feel like an idiot. After hearing Julian explain what was happening with Isadora, I wanted to crawl under a rock. I couldn't. I sat down at the dining room table with him and enjoyed a delicious dinner and a bottle of champagne.

By the time the chef and server were leaving, I was tipsy.

Julian took me home in a taxi and walked me to my door before kissing me goodnight. I thought he'd take me home with him, but that didn't happen.

I spent the night alone, wondering why I had allowed myself to get so jealous that I lost sight of what was right in front of me.

"I finally got in touch with that Simon guy," Jen interrupts my thoughts when she walks into my office. "He's interested in a second showing. I set that up for this afternoon. I emailed you a schedule for today."

I'm grateful that she's as aggressive as she is with chasing down leads.

I don't have much time left to sell the Bishop Hotel penthouse. When I first took on the job, I was certain that I'd have it sold in a week, but it's been a challenge.

It's made me realize that I don't have the same contacts as many of the other brokers at Carvel. Anne has encouraged everyone to work on this deal together, but they all know that if I fail that opens the door for another broker to take over.

It's smart business.

Why should they work their asses off to help me sell a property that they may end up selling on their own? It's no secret that the broker who lists the penthouse and sells it also gets the exclusive to the other eleven properties.

"Has anyone else called with an interest in seeing it?"

It's a useless question. Jen lets me know the instant anyone calls or emails about the penthouse.

"No one." She shrugs her shoulder. "I'm not giving up hope yet, Maya. We still have time and the Clarksons are super interested."

I'm starting to feel like they're my only remaining hope.

"I think it would be wise for us to start pursuing new listings." Jen looks down at her phone. "I've been sending out some queries to my old contacts to see if any of them are thinking about moving. We may be able to snag a listing or two through them."

I'm grateful. Jen knows that if I don't sell the penthouse that I'll have to let her go. Her salary is paid for by me, not Carvel and although I'm fine covering it now, I won't be able to afford it unless I earn that huge commission.

"I'll send out some emails to my contacts too." I pick up my phone. "I think that was all I needed."

"Don't give up, Maya." She steps closer to my desk. "You just sold a multi-million dollar property.

That's a huge accomplishment. Keep pushing on the penthouse and you'll get that sold too."

My eyes meet hers. "We'll get it sold. I couldn't do this without you."

She beams. "I'll get back to work. I'll send you a text reminder before your showing with Simon this afternoon."

***

"See how that works?" Julian ushers me into his office with a hand on the center of my lower back. "You tell my assistant you're here and she lets me know immediately."

I manage a smile. It took all the courage I could muster to come down here today and it wasn't just because I half expected to see Isadora following Julian around.

I have no idea if she's here or not. It doesn't matter. I had to see him after what happened last night. I turned what could have been a wonderful celebratory dinner into a difficult and awkward evening.

I wait until he closes the door behind me before I say anything. "I'm here to apologize. I didn't handle things well yesterday and I'm embarrassed."

He takes my face in his palms and plants a soft kiss on my lips. "It's forgotten, Maya."

I stare into his eyes. They're such a beautiful shade of blue. They match his tie to perfection today. That paired with the black shirt and suit he's wearing gives him an edgy, yet elegant look.

"I shouldn't have tested you like that." I want to put it behind me too, but not before he completely understands that I'm not normally the kind of person who tests someone she cares about. "I'm sorry that I did."

His hands glide down my neck to my shoulders. "I shouldn't have handled things the way I did either, but we're learning how to navigate one another, Maya. That's a good thing. It's healthy and important."

"You're incredible." I lean forward to kiss him. "I always thought you'd be the wisest person I'd ever met. You're proving me right."

"I'm far from wise." He steps back to unbutton his suit jacket. "I'm learning as I go."

I narrow my eyes as I consider his words. "I'm learning too. I'm learning that breaking my rules was one of the smartest choices I've ever made."

"Having dinner with me tonight would be a smart choice as well."

"As long as there are no alcoholic beverages involved, I'm on board." I roll my eyes. "I had way too much champagne last night."

"No drinks tonight," he agrees. "We'll have some dinner and then you'll show me what you have under that dress. I'll pick you up at your place at seven."

Chapter 32

Julian

"So you finally made your move?" Sebastian stretches his long legs as he sits on my couch. "It took you long enough."

I wait for a beat before replying because the joke holds more truth than I care to admit. I wasted time with Maya. When I first saw her at Falon Shaw's studio, I should have ended my relationship with Isadora that day.

I felt a pull to Maya that was unfamiliar. I wanted her in a way that I'd never wanted a woman before, but I assumed it was pure lust. Rearranging my entire life for a random fuck wasn't something I would have done then. I'd never consider it now either.

Isadora's decision to push me on the topic of marriage may have set the wheels in motion, but my desire for Maya was the catalyst for change.

I couldn't stay with Isadora when I wanted someone else as much as I did Maya.

"She's incredible, Sebastian." I take a seat on the chair next to the couch. "Getting to know her has changed me. It's changed my life."

"You sound like you're in love."

I consider his words carefully. I've wondered the same thing myself, but it's too soon. It feels too soon. "It's headed in that direction. I'm taking her to dinner in an hour."

"Good," he shoots back. "I want you happy. Which leads to my next question."

I cock a brow. "Ask away."

"Does Maya have a sister?"

Reaching forward I tap his knee with my hand. "Twins. She has twin sisters."

He shoots me a look. "I want details, Julian. Find out if they're single and make sure you tell them I'm NYPD. Women love that. They fucking love it."

***

"I thought you'd take me to Axel Tribeca." Maya closes the menu in front of her. "I like this place a lot though."

I didn't take her to Axel because I wanted to give her a new experience. That's why I brought her to this restaurant. It's small and they serve good Italian food. I can always get a table.

"Let's talk business for a minute." I rest my hands on top of the menu. "Tell me where you are with the penthouse sale."

She squeezes the side of her neck. "I have two interested parties and they both wanted a second showing. One of those happened today and the other is two days from now. I'm hopeful that I'll get an offer out of one of them."

I've kept a close eye on the calendar. I want to extend the deadline but I won't. We have a signed contract and granting her a favor because I'm dating her won't serve me well with the board. Beyond that, I'm confident that the penthouse will be off the market before the deadline arrives.

162

"You'll get it sold, Maya." I reach for her hand. "Second showings are a good sign of interest."

She looks down at our joined hands. "I believe that too. You met one of the parties. It's the Clarksons. Do you remember them?"

I'll never forget them. Dancing next to them is a sweet memory for me. That afternoon ended with me kissing Maya. The taste of her lips is something I crave. To satiate that, I lean forward and kiss her, softly.

"What was that for?"

"A thank you for dancing me with that day we met the Clarksons." I kiss her again. "That one is a thank you for later when you let me ravage your body in my bed."

"Is that what we are having for dessert?" she whispers. "You'll eat me before you fuck me?"

I move closer to her in the booth we're sitting in. "Is that what you want me to do?"

"Yes." She looks into my eyes. "I'm tempted to skip dinner and go straight to dessert. It's been days since I've felt you inside me."

I reach for her thigh and her lips part slightly. "Spread."

She does. She parts her knees and I take full advantage, skimming my fingertips up her leg until they rest under the hem of her white skirt.

"Do you want me inside you now?" I whisper the words against her lips before I claim her mouth in a deep kiss. "Tell me you do."

She eyes the only server in the place. His face is buried in his phone. The kitchen staff is out of view, and the only other patrons are seated clear across the restaurant. "I've never done…"

I slide my fingers to the edge of her panties. They're lace, likely pretty. I run my fingertip over the top of her leg where the panties meet her soft skin.

"I'll come." She half giggles, half moans. "I'll come if you touch me now."

She's so wet that I can feel it through the lace. "Then you'll come."

I skim my finger under the fabric and along the top of her mound. It's just as smooth as it was the last time I touched her. "Spread more."

There's no hesitation as she does. She shifts on the seat, pushing her legs far enough apart that it grants me access to her wetness.

I glide my finger over the seam of her pussy, slowly; painfully slowly and the moan that escapes her is caught in my mouth when I kiss her.

"If you come now, you blow me later."

"I'll crawl under the table and blow you now," she counters with a lift of her brow. "I love sucking your cock."

The need to be inside of her is strong. I want my dick in her heat, pounding into her with steady even strokes until I feel her shudder around me.

Since I can't have that, I take what I can, gliding my fingertips along the wetness until I find her clit.

I watch her intently as she bites her lip and her eyes roll back in her head. I circle that nub of plump swollen flesh with my finger, over and over, increasing the pressure, slowing and then racing, pushing her to the edge.

Her hips start to circle, small bursts of movement chasing after what she craves most right now. She wants to come here, next to me, because the need outweighs everything else.

"I told you… god, Julian, I'm going…"

I take her mouth again in a deep, messy kiss just as I shove two fingers inside her so I can feel every ripple of her tight pussy as she gives me her release.

Chapter 33

Maya

"How is it that no one in that restaurant noticed me having an orgasm?" I lean my head on his shoulder after we step into his apartment. "I would notice if someone was having an orgasm while I was eating spaghetti."

He laughs. "You tasted the spaghetti, Maya. It's phenomenal. It's easy to get swept away in the food and become oblivious to everything around you."

I hit his chest with a playful slap. "I've never done anything like that before."

"I haven't either." He reaches for my hand to bring it to his lips. "I couldn't wait. I had to be inside you and since everyone would have noticed if I spread you out and fucked you on the table next to the complimentary breadsticks, touching you quelled my need, temporarily."

"Temporarily?" I tap my finger on my chin. "Does that mean that I get to have my dessert soon?"

"Eating you out is my dessert, Maya." He slides his suit jacket off. "You're going to ride my face until you can't take it anymore."

"I can take a lot." I start to unbutton the red blouse I'm wearing just as his phone starts to ring.

He ignores it as he watches me push the blouse off to reveal the red bra underneath. "Leave that on when you mount me. I want to look up and see your tits covered in red lace."

His phone starts ringing again shortly after it stops.

"Answer your phone." I point at his jacket as I unzip the side zipper on my skirt. "It could be important."

He slides his jacket off and tosses it onto the floor. "Nothing is as important as your dessert."
I push down my skirt and watch his face. His eyes are trained on my panties. They're white lace with a red ribbon trim.

He steps forward and reaches out to finger the ribbon. I don't move. I can't. I crave this man's touch. "I knew they'd be pretty. Take them off, Maya and get in my bedroom."

I do. I drop my panties and let him take me to his bed.

***

"Can you dislocate your jaw by sucking on cock?" I rub my fingers over my jaw.

Julian pushes the sheet that's covering him lower to reveal his semi-hard dick. I have no clue how it can still have any life left in it. I sucked him to orgasm after I rode his face. Then he fucked me hard on his bed.

I can barely move, and he looks ready to go another round.

"Is it tender?" He skims his finger over my chin. "I'm sorry if I was too aggressive."

He was aggressive. He climbed on top of me and straddled my face. It was hot, so hot that I almost came when he fisted my hair and shoved his thick cock down my throat.

It was the first time I've gagged and that seemed to spur his drive even more. I let him use me while I held onto his powerful thighs. He pumped into me over and over until his release flooded my throat.

"It was perfect." I sigh. "We'll do that again?"

His face brightens. "Anytime."

"Not tonight." I open and close my mouth twice. "Give it a day or two to heal."

His lips skim over my jawline. "Thank you for tonight, Maya. All of it."

I know that cue. I've heard it in the past. Not from him, but still. When a man wants a woman out the door, he'll thank her politely for the sex and then help her get dressed.

I start to roll to my side. "I'll have to find my clothes. I'm not sure where my panties are."

"Under my pillow." He scoops his hand under the pillow his head is resting on and tugs out my red and white panties. "I'm keeping these."

"You're going to send me home with a bare pussy?" I pretend to scowl. "I hope it's not windy. My skirt doesn't behave in a breeze."

He furrows his brow. "I'm not sending you anywhere and I might keep the skirt too to make certain that you never give another peep show to the random men of Manhattan on windy days."

"You're not sending me home?"

"I want you to spend the night." He tugs me closer to him. "Sleep in my arms, fuck me in the shower tomorrow, let me make you breakfast."

"I want to do all of that." I nuzzle my cheek into his chest. "I won't go anywhere."

"Good." He rests his chin on the top of my head. "I want you to sleep, Maya. Close your eyes and dream about me."

"I do that every night," I say softly. "I have for years."

Chapter 34

Maya

This is it. I'm showing the penthouse to the Clarksons again. They are my last hope.

When I showed it to Simon the other day, there was no excitement in his eyes. He walked through the space sullenly, not asking any additional questions. He left in a hurry, and I haven't heard anything from him or his representative, Todd, since then.

I hear the ding of the elevator and I smooth my hands over the blue dress I'm wearing. It's a simple sheath dress. I've pulled my hair back into a tight ponytail, and I've applied the barest hint of makeup.

I did all of that while texting Julian this morning. As I was leaving his place yesterday morning, he told me that he'd be consumed with work for the next few days. I didn't take it as a brush off. I heard his phone ringing periodically through the night as I tried to sleep.

He's opening a new hotel in Paris soon and with everything else he's trying to juggle, that has to put even more stress on him.

Isadora might be part of every decision he makes right now, but she's not the one who spent the night with him. I am. I feel more confident in his feelings for me after the intimacy we shared.

"Maya," Irene Clarkson approaches me as they round the corridor and enter the main living space. "You look beautiful."

"Thank you." I step toward her when I sense that she's coming in for an embrace. She does. "You look rested and well, Irene. Tom's been treating you extra well?"

Tom leans forward to kiss my cheek softly. "I treasure this woman. I make every single day as special as I can."

This is what I want with Julian. I'm falling in love with him. I haven't admitted that to anyone yet, but my heart is screaming it constantly. It's much too soon to tell him, so I'll hold onto the feeling myself until the time is right to share it.

"How's Julian?" Irene bumps her shoulder against mine. "He's a handsome fellow, Maya. I think he runs a close second to Tom."

I smile at her. "Julian is well. He's caught up in work but that's what happens when you run one of the premier hotel chains in the country."

"Speaking of that." Tom wraps his arm around Irene's shoulders. "We have to thank him for the spa day and dinner at Axel. What a treat that was. The man certainly knows how to treat his guests."

And his lovers.

I'm still nursing a tender ache in virtually every one of my muscles after our marathon night. Once I finally did fall asleep, I woke to the wet heat of Julian's tongue on my nipple. He licked me to an early morning orgasm before he took me in the shower from behind.

I left his apartment more satisfied than I've ever felt and more sure of his devotion to me.

"If all goes well, maybe we can meet him for a drink." I wink.

"We love this place." Irene looks toward the bank of windows directly in front of us. "We've worked hard for a retirement that includes a place just like this."

Those words are music to my ears.

I sweep my arm in the air. "I want you both to take your time and look around. I've arranged lunch to be delivered on the terrace for you so you can get a feel for that. Cut a rug here in the main room if you'd like. Just see if this place connects with the two of you and your vision for the future."

Irene's eyes well with tears. "You are a dear. It's a big decision. We want to be sure."

"As you should be." I squeeze her hand. "I'm going to be in the office down the hall doing a bit of work. If you have any questions or you need to hear a little Sinatra, let me know."

They both smile as I wave my phone in the air.

"Thank you, Maya." Tom takes in a deep breath. "We think we know what we want to do, but this opportunity will settle those nerves for us."

I feel my heart leap. They're close. I think this might be it.

"I'll leave you two to enjoy the space together." I walk away with a feeling that the Clarksons just found their New York home.

***

"You had an interview with Julian today?" I motion for Charlie to close my office door. "For what?"

He shuts the door behind him before he settles in one of the guest chairs in front of my desk. "Senior counsel for Bishop Hotels."

That's Isadora's job.

"I know what you're thinking, Maya." He crosses his legs. "He's getting rid of Isadora."

I smile at his choice of words. I'd like to get rid of her too. If I had my choice, she'd be on an airplane headed to some remote location that doesn't have any return flights.

"Did he say when you'd start this job if he offers it to you?" I push because I'm curious.

Julian and I haven't discussed Isadora since the day after I saw her at his office. I've been tempted to ask about their involvement on business projects, but that would cause friction between us that isn't necessary.

I know Julian cares deeply for me and that Isadora is just a co-worker. At least, in his eyes that's the case, I obviously can't begin to imagine how she views him.

"About a month from now." He slides his fingers along the arm of his glasses. "I haven't told Anne yet, or anyone for that matter. I know you're involved with Julian now that he's no longer with Isadora. I thought you'd like to know that I may be working with him soon."

Charlie and I haven't discussed my relationship with Julian because we've both moved on. He's been dating the woman from accounting. I've seen the two of them together in the breakroom. He's happy and I'm glad for that.

Our connection may have been brief, but I want him to find the same kind of fulfillment that I'm finding with Julian.

"I appreciate that," I offer with a small smile. "Has Isadora left Bishop?"

"No." He shakes his head. "I had to meet Julian at the hotel in Tribeca for a coffee. He didn't want me at the office. He said Isadora wasn't aware that he was interviewing and he wanted me to keep it quiet. He told me that Isadora talked to him about hiring me on as a junior attorney before they broke up."

"Really?"

"I was surprised too but he said that's why she invited me to the launch party." He stops to scratch his chin." I don't think he'll mind that I'm telling you all of this."

I don't think he will either, but I'm mildly surprised that he didn't mention it to me already. We shared a string of text messages this morning, but those were mostly flirtatious offerings.

"Will you take it, Charlie?" I ask with a grin playing on my lips. I already know the answer. Charlie's potential isn't being utilized here at Carvel. He spends most of his time reviewing sales contracts and working on closing documents.

He told me during our first date that he wants more challenge to sink his teeth into. Working at Bishop will give him that.

"In a heartbeat, Maya." He holds up his hand, showing me two crossed fingers. "Keep your fingers crossed for me. Or better yet, put in a good word with Julian. I want that job, Maya. I really want it."

Chapter 35

Julian

"You're killing two birds with one stone." Sebastian draws a pull from the beer in front of him. He rarely drinks, so I know he's on edge.

"That's irony." Griffin sits on the arm of my sofa. "Sebastian talking about killing with a stone. Isn't that how…"

"Shut up." Sebastian throws him a look. "I'm behind you, Julian. You know that. I don't like that you're doing favors for Isadora or that asshole, but I get it. You want her out and this is the way to make it happen."

I do want her out of the business. I want her out of my life period, but that's a process. She's behaved herself over the course of the past few days since she's come back to work. I avoid her and she only bothers me if it's a work-related matter.

She still has no idea that I'm seeing Maya. I haven't told her because I want to spare Maya her wrath. There's zero doubt in my mind that Isadora would seek Maya out and give her an earful if she knew how I felt about her.

"It's brilliant." Griffin stands. "I'm all about this. I have no idea how you pulled this out of your hat, Julian, but it's impressive."

It is but only if every piece falls into place. So far, it's worked out beautifully and as soon as I'm certain that Isadora has signed her new employment contract, I can tell Maya.

"We should celebrate the fact that one of us has a woman worth all of this." Griffin picks up his empty beer bottle. "Julian's in love. He's actually in fucking love this time."

"She has twin sisters," Sebastian quips. "Twins, Griffin. One for me and one for you."

"Do they look like her?" Griffin cocks a brow. "I checked out Maya's profile on her work website and that's a beautiful woman."

I smile. "She's gorgeous, inside and out."

"Introduce us to these twins." Griffin squares his shoulders. "Make that happen."

"One is married. She lives back in San Francisco. She has two kids."

He rolls his hand in the air. "Get to the other one. Where can I find her?"

I tell him everything I know about Matilda Baker. I gleaned that from searching online late last night when I was craving more information about Maya's life before she met me. Social media can reveal a person's soul if they're not careful.

"She's eighteen months younger than Maya. She works at Premier Pet Care here in Manhattan."

"I'm out." Griffin taps his chest. "I'm allergic to animals."

Sebastian laughs. "I'll meet her when I meet her. Work is a bitch right now. When the fuck do I have time for a woman?"

***

"To what do I owe this surprise?" Maya stares at my hands as I stand in the doorway of her office. "Is this a flower delivery?"

"It is." I move forward with the bouquet of two dozen pink roses in my hand. "It's for Maya Baker."

She pushes back from her desk and stands. The sight of her body wrapped in a hot pink dress almost drops me on the spot. "I'm Maya. I suppose you're expecting a tip."

I smile. "The last delivery I made was pizza and I don't know if you can top that tip."

Her tongue flicks over her bottom lip. "I can top it."

"If only I had the time right now." I rub the front of my trousers over my hardness. "I can't look at you and not get hard."

She moves closer and reaches for the flowers. "You say that as if it's a problem, Julian."

A grin floats over my lips. "It's never going to be a problem. If we could somehow run our businesses naked, in bed, I'd be a happy man."

"I love these." She lifts the flowers to her nose and inhales. "They're breathtaking. Is it a special occasion?"

"I wanted to see your smile. I thought these would do the trick."

She peppers my cheek with light kisses before she goes in for a long, lingering kiss on my lips. "Your face does the trick. I can't look at you and not smile."

"You're an angel." I kiss her again before I let her go. "Tell me about your day."

She takes the flowers to her desk and gingerly places them down. "There's a vase in the breakroom. I'm going to steal it and put these in water."

"Before you do that," I begin as I step to block her exit from her office. "Have you had any new interest in the penthouse?"

She blows out a huff of air. "I know that I only have a few days left. I'm still trying. I want this sale."

I clear my throat, wishing I could tell her right now what I'm planning on doing. It would take the weight of the world off her shoulders. "There's still time."

"I wish it would stop for a few days." She rubs her forehead. "I've worked so hard for this and I've invested so much."

She has, in so many ways. This project has consumed her life for the past month. In addition to that, she's sold the Warton place and jumped headfirst into a relationship with me.

"It's not over until it's over, right?" she asks in a lighter tone. "I'm not giving up until the clock strikes midnight on the very last day."

Chapter 36

Maya

"You're not saying anything." I bump Julian's shoulder with my hand. "You don't like it, do you?"

I asked him to meet me at my apartment after work. I brought the flowers home with me and put them in a vase that is currently sitting in the middle of my dining room table. They are the only bright spot in the room.

"I'm a shit interior designer." I manage a small nervous laugh. "It's a work in progress."

He looks down at me with a curve of his lips. "Why is it that when I imagine you at home, it looks nothing like this?"

"Because this isn't how I imagine it in my mind either." I motion toward the white couch I bought last year. It was one of my first large furniture purchases. I assumed it was perfect because it's neutral , but it adds absolutely no character at all to the room.

He doesn't move from where he's standing near the entryway. "Explain that statement to me."

Anxiety bolts through me. I've never confessed to anyone that I'm not completely happy with my apartment. "I had a lot of ideas about what I wanted in a property before I became a broker."

"Go on." He encourages me with a hand on my shoulder.

I let out a shaky breath. "When it came time to buy my first place, I thought more about investment value than comfort. I didn't put a lot of thought into whether I enjoyed the space. I looked at it from a strictly financial viewpoint."

"So, you purchased this apartment because of the eventual return you'll receive when you sell?"

"Exactly." I give him a curt nod. "I got it for a fair price and with some time, I believe it will increase in value. I'll sell and move into something else."

He runs his fingers from my shoulder up to the base of my neck. I shiver at his touch. This is the first time he's been inside my apartment. I invited him to meet me here so I could give him more of a glimpse into my world, but I'm suddenly feeling like I'm revealing even more of myself to him than I intended.

"Is your plan to move into something that has the most potential for return?"

It's a fair question and highly likely that I'll do just that. I understand the real estate market in Manhattan. I can predict, with some certainty, which neighborhoods will see an uptick in property value. If I can stay ahead of the trends, I can pocket some serious cash, just from moving every few years.

"It's hard not to view real estate from that place when it's your life," I half-joke.

His lips part as he considers carefully what he wants to say. "It's not your entire life, Maya. You need a place to go to at the end of the day that feels like home. Does this feel like home to you?"

I don't hesitate at all. "No, it doesn't. It feels like a place to sleep."

I look around the apartment. It would make anyone happy to live here. The windows are bright and airy. The kitchen is well equipped. There are two spacious bedrooms and just as many bathrooms.

"What do you imagine my home looks like?" I turn to look directly at him. "You said that when you imagine me at home it looks nothing like this."

Silence fills the air before he answers. "You may not be ready to hear this, but if I'm completely honest, when I imagine you at home, it's with me, at my place."

I close my eyes and lean in close to his chest. "I am ready to hear it. It felt like home the first time I was there."

A deep laugh rumbles through his body. "I won't ask you to move in with me, yet, but I will one day. I promise I will one day."

I'll hold him to that promise, one day.

***

"My bed feels more like home." I look down at him as I move slowly over his cock. "It actually feels like heaven right now."

"Yes," he hisses the word across his tongue. "Ride me like that."

I up the tempo, but only slightly. I'm enjoying this too much. I've never been on top of him like this, with his cock buried so deep that pain has morphed into pleasure.

His hands slide over my skin to my breasts. He squeezes them softly before he pulls one of my nipples between his fingers and twists it. Hard.

I let out a low moan and grind down on his cock.

"Is that all it takes to get you to ride me hard?" He asks in a dangerously low tone.

I slow again, enjoying the easy movements. "We can take it slow tonight."

"How the fuck am I supposed to take it slow when your pussy has my cock in its grip?" He pushes my hips down onto him. "Fuck me harder, Maya. Just fuck me."

I don't. I slow the pace even more, barely moving as I lean down to trace his lips with the tip of my tongue. "Take it slow, Julian."

He growls. It's an animalistic sound of need mixed with pure desire. "Slow is good, but tonight I need to fuck hard."

I scream when he flips me onto my back and dives his head between my legs. He eats me wildly, nipping at the tender flesh of my core as I wiggle beneath him.

"You're a tease." He pants as he licks slow circles over my clit. "It's your turn to be teased."

He pushes two thick fingers inside of me, probing, taking, finding that spot that he knows is going to take me to the brink.

It does. I cry out that I'm close but he chuckles and pulls back.

He stretches so he's on his knees over me, looking down, my slick-soaked fingers in his mouth.

"I'll let you come when I do." He teases my entrance with the swollen sheath covered head of his cock. "I'll fuck you how I want tonight, and then when you come, I'll fuck you how you want."

"Fuck me hard." I writhe on the bed. "Fuck me until I scream."

He does. He drives his cock into me in one violent, sudden motion. I fist the sheets of my bed and moan on every deep thrust until we come at the very same time.

Chapter 37

Julian

"I don't bathe, Maya. I shower."

"Has anyone ever told you that sometimes you sound like a stuck up snob?" She pours pink bubble bath under the running water.

I slide a finger down her bare back until I reach her ass. I give that a sharp smack.

"Um, ow." She rubs the now red skin with her palm as she casts a glance over her shoulder at me. "That hurt."

"It made you wet."

A blush creeps across her cheeks. "Maybe a little."

"In answer to your question, yes. My friend, Sebastian, tells me I'm a stuck up prick sometimes," I admit.

"I like him." She places the bottle of bubble bath back in a cabinet that's hanging on the wall. "Can I meet him?"

"He'd love to meet you." I don't add that he'd like to meet her sister as well because I need Sebastian in my life and if he fucked things up with Maya's sister, I might have to choose sides, and I'd choose her without question.

"Does he work for Bishop too?" Her blue eyes sparkle as she asks me.

We're both nude, standing in the middle of her washroom and I've never felt more comfortable with anyone in my life.

"Sebastian works for the NYPD. Homicide division," I say it with pride.

I'm very proud of how far both Sebastian and Griffin have come. They set out on their chosen paths after high school and charted the course they wanted. My sister's fiancé, Smith Booth, has done the same. We've been friends for years as well, and soon we'll be brothers-in-law.

"He sounds like a big deal." She grabs my forearm as she steps into the bathtub. "I want you to meet people who are important to me too. Falon is my best friend and Tilly, my sister, she lives in Manhattan. You should meet her."

I follow her in, settling into the warm water behind her so she can rest her back against my chest. I smooth the hair from her neck. "I want to know everything about you, Maya. I want to meet all the people you love."

Her hands float over my legs. "This feels so right. Doesn't this feel right, Julian?"

"It feels like home."

***

"Who is she?" Isadora steps out of the shadows as I approach my building.

I left Maya so she could finally sleep. I can see the exhaustion on her face, and after our bath, I rubbed lotion into her skin and helped her get under the covers. She was fading away before I kissed her goodnight and left.

"Why are you here?" I stop in place. "You need to leave."

She stands her ground, not moving at all. "You left me for someone else, didn't you?"

"I left you because I don't love you and you deserve more, Isadora."

I mean that. It likely sounds like a load of bullshit to her, but I mean that. After realizing what it's like to actually fall in love with someone, how can I not hope that she finds that too? Just because we weren't right for each other, doesn't mean she won't find happiness and fulfillment with another man.

"Were you sleeping with her when you were with me?"

I hate this. I fucking hate drama.

"I never cheated on you." I blow out a puff of air into the cool evening sky. "I was faithful."

She swallows hard as she looks down at her hands. "I want to believe that, Julian. I need to because right now I feel like shit inside knowing that you're dating another woman."

I have no idea how she's figured that out, but it's out there. Thankfully, she doesn't realize it's Maya.

"Is there a chance that things will change?" I hear the desperate note of hopelessness in her voice. "Maybe you're just sowing your oats and when you're done, you'll come back to me."

Like any wound, it's best to rip the bandage off, so the pain is fleeting. "There's no chance."

"Is that it? We're done forever?"

"We're done," I say firmly. "Live your life, Isadora. Chase your own happiness."

She wraps her arms around her waist. "I don't know how, Julian. I don't know how."

I wave down an approaching taxi. "Take it one day at a time. You'll find your way. I can't be there to help you anymore."

I see the resignation in her face as she turns toward the taxi. "I don't think I can do this, Julian. I need you. You're all I have left."

There's more. She can't see it yet, but she will. She has to. I pray that she does.

Chapter 38

Maya

As soon as I got into my office this morning, I was on the phone. I called several of my former clients to see if they had thought about moving. I pointed out the benefits of living in a residence hotel, but every reply was the same. They couldn't afford it.

I'm back at the penthouse now. I thought if I took a few minutes to stand in it, inspiration might hit me. It hasn't.

As I scoop up my purse on my way out, my phone starts ringing. I answer it immediately, not bothering to check who is calling. I'm at the point of desperation where I'm tempted to answer with a sales pitch about the property.

"This is Maya Baker," I say cheerfully with a roll of my eyes.

"Maya? It's Todd Bolton. We met several weeks ago when I toured the Bishop Hotel property."

"Of course." I settle into one of the dining room chairs. "My client is prepared to make an offer if the property is still available."

I feel tears welling in the corner of my eyes, but I keep my tone controlled and professional. "That's great news, Todd."

"He'll be purchasing it through one of his holding companies so the documentation I'm sending will bear that name and my signature."

Sure, sure, whatever. As long as I sell the place, I don't care who owns it.

"I'm sending our offer and conditions via courier to your office this afternoon." He shuffles with something that sounds like papers. "Present it to your client and let us know as soon as possible."

"I will." I bounce to my feet. "I'm heading to my office now."

"Maya." His voice lowers. "I want to make one thing very clear. This is our best and final offer. We're not prepared to negotiate. It's a take it or leave it situation."

I close my eyes. That doesn't bode well for me. Julian has made it clear that he wants as close to list price as possible. Whenever someone says they won't negotiate, it generally means they are offering something well below asking.

"I'll speak to my client, Todd, and then I'll be in touch."

I end the call and stand in silence. This is the only offer I have. It better be good enough to please Julian because if it's not, another broker will get the sale and I'll get nothing.

***

"I'm calling the Clarksons." I look over at Jen. "I know they can beat this."

"You should be calling Julian to tell him that you have an offer," she points out. "You know he'll reject it, Maya. It's too low."

That's what I'm afraid of. I have exactly twelve hours left to secure a contract for the property and if I take Todd's offer to Julian, he'll refuse it which will leave me out of the running for the rest of the residential suites.

"No law says I can't use Todd's offer as leverage." I scroll through my phone's contact list looking for the Tom Clarkson's number. "I'm going to be honest with Tom and Irene. I'll tell him that I have an offer and if they're interested in the property they need to act now."

"Do it." She nods at my phone. "I hope to hell it works, Maya. I've loved working for you."

"You love working for me," I correct her. "I'm not sending you packing yet."

As she's leaving I dial Tom's number, but he doesn't pick up, so I leave a voicemail asking him to give me a call at his earliest convenience. Once I've done that I thumb out a text message to him essentially saying the same thing. I add to it that it's time sensitive with the hope that I'll hear back from him within the hour.

A faint knock on the doorframe of my office draws my attention up. "I don't have an appointment but do you think you can fit me in?"

"Falon." I greet her with a warm smile as I push back from my desk. "What are you doing here?"

She moves to hug me. I take advantage, wrapping my arms around her before I finally step back.

"Checking to see if you're still alive." She pushes my hair back over my shoulders. "I'm worried about you. I know that your window to sell the penthouse is almost up."

"I have time." I sigh heavily. "Not a lot, but I'm hopeful that I can present Julian with an acceptable offer before my time runs out."

"Tilly told me that you two had gotten close." She eyes me up. "I should have heard about that before her."

She's right. I know she doesn't feel any jealousy toward my sister. I've long considered Falon more of a sister to me than either of my biological siblings, but she knows that I'm trying to close the gap between Tilly and me. It's one of the reasons why I introduced them to each other months ago.

"I should have told you."

"Tilly was happy to. I don't care how I found out because I'm thrilled for you." She looks me straight in the eyes. "Is he good to you, Maya?"

"The best," I answer quickly. "I've never known anyone like him. I think he might be it for me."

She won't judge. Falon would never tell me that it's too soon to feel what I'm feeling. She fell for Asher just as quickly and now they're inseparable.

"I'm around for a few more weeks." Her head whips back when she hears a loud conversation filtering in through the open doorway. "Call me if you need a pep talk or just to vent about work. You've got a lot on your plate right now."

"I can handle it." I give her another hug. "I've got everything under control."

Chapter 39

Julian

I've been expecting this call all day, and frankly, I was growing concerned when Maya didn't reach out by mid-afternoon. I held my breath and checked my phone repeatedly waiting for her to get in touch. She has only a few hours left before the contract she signed expires and I go in search of another broker.

I checked in with Anne Carvel earlier in the day. She was the one who informed me that an offer had been made. I was tempted to text Maya to ask if there had been any activity, but this is her deal, and how she approaches it is entirely up to her.

"Maya," I answer on the second ring. "How are you?"

"Happy," she responds quickly. "First things first, you're an incredible lover."

I chuckle as I glance out at my deserted office. It's been hours since my assistant left. Some of the other executives hung back until the early evening, but they've all since gone home.

"You know how I feel about your lovemaking skills, Maya. I'm blown away."

That brings a bubble of laughter over the line. "If our meeting goes well, a blowjob may be in your very near future."

Blurring the line between business and pleasure has never bothered me. It does now. I want this deal to happen because it would be beneficial to us both. If anything goes wrong, it could impact us in a very personal way.

"Do we have a meeting scheduled?"

"I called your assistant but she'd left for the day so I penciled myself in for ten p.m."

I glance down at the clock on my desk. I rub my forehead trying to ease the stress. "I should expect you within the next ten minutes?"

"You should expect me now, handsome. I'm early. Look up."

I do. I see my beautiful Maya, with a leather briefcase in her hand and every expectation in the world in her eyes.

***

"Why are we in the conference room?" She surveys the long wooden table with the dozen chairs surrounding it. "Is someone else joining us?"

I place my hand on her lower back to guide her to the chair next to the head of the table where I'll be seated. "I wanted us to be more comfortable. My desk is a mess and this room affords us more space."

She doesn't respond but waits patiently as I pull out the chair before she sits.

I take the seat next to her and clear my throat. "What are we meeting about? Do you have an offer?"

"I do." She reaches down to grab her briefcase, clicking the cover open with her thumb. "It's lower than what you were looking for, but I feel it's a solid offer."

She pulls an offer form from the case and slides it across the table to me. I skim it, taking note of the buyer which is a company, the offer, and the terms.

"You can see that it's a solid offer. It's a million less than ask and I know that you were set on the price, but you have to consider what comparable properties in the city are selling for," she pauses. "I understand that those don't come with the same amenities as the penthouse but you're getting one of the highest cost per square foot that Chelsea has ever seen."

I want to tell her to stop. I look down at the paper, scanning the details although none of them are sinking in.

"Maya." I slide the paper forward on the desk. "It's a good offer."

"You think it's a good offer?" Her eyes brighten.

I stumble with what to say next. I've been anticipating this for some time. I've worked hard behind the scenes to secure this deal. I feel like shit right now that I'm not confessing that to her but I want her to have this sale so she can shine with the additional eleven units all on her own.

I finger the edge of the document as I look around the room.

"I need a moment, Maya." I start to push back from the table, unease settling over me. "I have to clear my head."

Her hand on my forearm stops me. "Don't go. I have something else to show you."

I love the flirtation but I can't even look her in the eye right now. "It will need to wait."

"It can't wait." She reaches down into her bag again and fumbles for something. I watch her every move until another paper appears in her hand.

"I also have this." She slides a second offer sheet across the table toward me and my stomach clenches into a tight knot. "Full ask, no contingences, thirty day close and all cash."

Fuck.

I scrub my hands over my face. It's so fucking impressive that I'm at a loss for words.

"I received the second offer less than an hour ago." She tugs on the corner of the offer sheet. "It's from Tom and Irene Clarkson. They want to spend the rest of their lives there, dancing their nights away, drinking their morning coffee on the terrace."

"I can't accept it." My voice sounds foreign, broken and sullen.

"What?" She laughs. "You can't accept what?"

"The Clarksons." I don't look at her. "I'm accepting the other offer, Maya."

I know what that means to her. The lost extra commission and the call she'll have to make to Tom and Irene explaining that their ideal offer was rejected.

"You're not making sense." She pushes the offer sheet toward me again. "This offer is exactly what you wanted. You have to take it."

"I can't take it." I push it back at her. "I'm accepting the other offer."

Chapter 40

Maya

I sit in stunned silence. I can't wrap my mind around what's happening. I just presented Julian with two offers for the penthouse, and he wants to accept the weaker of the two. It's less money, horrible terms and a ninety-day close.

"I deserve an explanation." I look at him, but he's facing the doorway. "I worked my ass off to sell that place, and something isn't adding up."

"Senator Carney is behind that shell corporation." He throws his head back against the chair. "I made a deal with him, Maya. He's giving me something in exchange for the reduced price on the penthouse."

That feels like a boot to the stomach. Not only am I missing out on a nice chunk of commission but Julian is essentially telling me that he pre-negotiated this deal. I had no real part in it which means technically I didn't sell the property.

I've been wasting my time trying to sell an apartment that he'd already agreed to sell.

"What is he giving you?" I spit the words out in anger. "What the hell is he giving you that is worth that much?"

"Freedom." He pushes back and stands.

I know who Senator Carney is and I know for a fact that he didn't tour the penthouse with me. Both Todd and Simon are too young to be the senator.

Neither of them mentioned anything about him. My head is spinning in confusion.

Senator Carney's son, Bert, was accused of killing a man. He beat the victim's face in with a rock until he was completely unrecognizable and then he got off on some technicality. I dated his lawyer briefly which is how I know so much about the case. Everett, Bert's attorney, couldn't shut up about it. I was so appalled that I left him during dinner one night without another word.

"Does this have to do with that murder case?" I ask quietly. "You're not involved in that, Julian, are you?"

"Fuck, no." He finally looks at me. "Maya, no. I would never. "

"What then?" I push to my feet. "You said you were buying your freedom. What does that mean?"

"I need Isadora gone. She admires the senator, so I put out some feelers to see if he had a position for her. He called me and asked what I could offer in exchange. I told him I wouldn't deal that way, but then he became aware of the penthouse and expressed an interest in it."

"That's illegal." I sit back down. "Isn't it bribery or something?"

"No." He shakes his head. "I had two lawyers look it over, Maya. It's all above board."

Two lawyers. Two people who knew about this when I didn't have a clue.

"All of this to get Isadora out of the picture?" I shake my head. It's unreasonable and extreme. Granted, I don't like her, but there has to be a solution beyond him selling me out.

"I want her to start a new life away from here." He folds his arms over his chest. "She'd relocate to Washington. The past would finally be in the past and you and I can move forward without the threat of her over us."

"She's just an ex-girlfriend." I try and laugh it off. "She'll get over you eventually. It doesn't matter if she's sitting in the office next to you or in an office in D.C."

"You don't know her the way I do, Maya."

"I'm a woman. I know what it feels like to have my heart broken by someone I love." I hate dredging up my past but I feel the need to. "I wasn't ready to let go of my ex either, Julian."

"You're nothing like Isadora." He clenches his hands into tight fists. "She was waiting for me outside my apartment the other night. She wanted to know who I was fucking. She will push and push until she pushes you away."

I finally see things clearly. This isn't all about his freedom from Isadora. This is about his fear of losing me.

"If you sign off on that deal, you are only prolonging the inevitable." My voice rises out of pure frustration. "She'll go to Washington and pine for you from afar. She'll still look at your social media accounts every day and pick apart every single post. She'll call you for no reason but to hear your voice. Sending her away won't change anything, Julian."

"It will give me breathing room." The exasperation in his tone is evident. "I don't expect you to understand any of this, Maya. How could you?"

"I lived it," I say softly. "I was just like Isadora once."

***

I sip the glass of water he got me. He hasn't said anything since I told him that I was like Isadora. I know he's waiting for an explanation and I have to give him one. I suck in a deep breath because this is going to take all the courage I possess.

"I moved to New York City because of a man."

Unease floats over his expression. He's sitting again now, next to me. He's stoic and silent.

"I fell in love with a man in San Francisco. He was the man I told you about."

"The man who left you for his ex." It's a statement, not a question. "I assumed that ended when he left you."

"It should have." I clench my hands together on the table. "I loved him or felt that I did at the time. I wasn't willing to accept his decision."

"So you followed him to New York?"

"I followed him and his wife to New York," I clarify. "I couldn't breathe knowing he was in a different state so I packed up my things and came here. I rented a small apartment and applied to college. I found a part-time job."

"Was he aware that you followed him across the country?" There's no readable inflection in his voice at all. I can't tell what he's thinking or feeling.

I shift in my seat, the restless energy I feel gnawing at me. "I sought him out often. I showed up at his work, followed him when he took her out. I essentially stalked them both."

It's difficult to admit. I was damn lucky at the time that neither of them called the police. If they had, my life would be much different.

"Why, Maya?" He studies my face. "Why did you do it?"

I hold his gaze while I answer. "I thought he was the only man I'd ever love. I wanted him with such force that it obliterated all common sense. I was determined to be the one he chose. I'd convinced myself that he'd realize his mistake and come back to me, so in my mind, being in New York made sense."

"How was this resolved?"

I chuckle because I could never have predicted the outcome. "I eventually gave up because he made it clear repeatedly that I was not the woman for him."

"Does he live here? Do you ever seek him out now?" He leans forward to rest both elbows on the table.

"I have no idea where he is now. I don't care." I look at the documents on the table. "The last time I saw him was years ago. He'd heard I was a rental agent and he needed a place to live. He split from his wife and he came to me."

I take a deep breath and go on, "I didn't feel a thing for him anymore but he told me he loved me and wanted me back."

His eyebrows lift with a silent question, so I answer it.

"I told him I didn't love him anymore and I couldn't help him."

"He's the reason why you made me promise to tell you if I was considering getting back together with Isadora?"

"I'm older now. I understand love more." I smile softly. "I didn't ask you to tell me because I was worried that I'd end up chasing you to the ends of the earth to get you back. I asked you so that I could give myself the necessary time to grieve and to let go in a healthy way."

I can tell he's waiting for me to say more, but when I don't, he responds. "That's a very mature approach to take, Maya. I understand more now why you tested me that day in my office."

"I slipped into fear that day," I admit. "I recognized it quickly. That's why I told you and why I wanted you to understand how deeply sorry I was for how I behaved."

"You've given me a lot to think about." He scrubs his hand over the back of his neck.

I huff out a laugh. "I hope I didn't scare you away, but I wanted you to know about my past and the person I am now."

Chapter 41

Julian

I stare at the two offer sheets in front of me. One is a result of Maya's hard work and dedication. The other is the result of my selfish need to push my past as far away as I can.

"Julian?" Maya says my name from where she's standing near the doorway.

She'd left to freshen up and to give me space to absorb everything she told me about her past. I was surprised and confused, but also grateful that she opened up the way that she did. It helps me understand her and the way she loves.

It changes absolutely nothing about my feelings. If anything I care more deeply about her. It took courage to be that vulnerable. I admire her for that.

"Yes?" I turn in my chair to look at her.

"Let Isadora find her path." She takes a step toward me. "I know I have no right to suggest anything here, but you want her to find a life that is fulfilling for her, so give her a chance to do that. If you still want me, I know I can deal with her. Together, you and I are stronger than her pain."

"I want you, Maya." I push myself to my feet. "I'm in love with you."

"I'm in love with you too." Tears well in her eyes. "This time it's real. I can tell."

"How can you tell?" I go to her and wipe the tears from her cheeks with the pad of my thumb.

She wraps her arms around my waist as she stares into my eyes. "If you told me today that you didn't love me and that you wanted to find your happiness, I'd let you go because I love you enough to want that for you."

I swallow past the lump in my throat. "I can't say that I'd do the same, Maya. Now, that I have you, I'll never let you go."

"Don't let go then." She rises to her tiptoes to kiss my jaw. "Hold me forever."

"That's my intention." I claim her mouth with a soft kiss. "I want this to be my forever."

***

"I don't expect you to make a decision tonight." Maya picks up her briefcase. "You have a lot to consider and I can't tell you what will or won't work with Isadora. I don't want this decision to come back to haunt us in the future."

"Do you have a pen?" I hold out my hand.

She fishes inside her purse and finally pulls out a blue pen. "Here's one. Are you going to accept an offer?"

"The clock is running out, Maya." I point to her wrist. "If I don't sign one of these by midnight, your contract with Bishop will be null and void."

She looks at the watch on her wrist. "This says it's three a.m., but I don't own a watch that tells the actual time."

I laugh. "You'll have to explain that to me sometime."

"Anytime." Her eyes fall to her phone's screen. "We have thirty minutes to spare."

"I'm proud of you." I rest the pen on the table. "I've never been more proud of anyone in my life."

A smile tugs at her mouth. "Coming from you that means everything, Julian."

I look down at the two offer sheets again.

"I need to thank you for taking this chance on me." She slicks her tongue over her bottom lip. "It's been a challenging month, and my stress levels have been off the charts, but I know, without a doubt, that this is what I'm supposed to be doing. I love this job. I love everything about it and now, I have more drive than I've ever had before."

"You're one of the best brokers in this city," I say that with sincerity. "You're going to have a long and very successful career."

"This is just the beginning." She leans her hip against the table before she smooths her hand over the skirt of her red dress. "I have two new listing appointments for later this week and I have another two clients who are set to sell in late summer, so I'm going to be okay."

"You have a pretty great boyfriend." I point out with a grin. "He's going to ask you to move in with him soon."

Her eyes drop to the offer sheets. "I'll say yes to that. He's a keeper."

I pick up the pen. "One day after you move in, he'll tell you he wants to marry you."

Her voice softens. "I'll tell him I want to marry him too."

I hold the pen in the air. "He'll do his best to make every one of your dreams come true."

Her hand on my forearm stops me. "Listen to your heart, Julian. You told me to do that and I'm asking you now to do the same. I'll accept your decision, whatever it is."

I want there to be no doubt in her mind about what I'm about to do. I want her to know instinctively that I will put her first, always. Protecting her may have been the driving force behind my effort to negotiate a deal that would remove Isadora from my life, but I won't allow my ex-girlfriend to dictate my decisions anymore.

I kiss Maya tenderly before I sign on the dotted line, agreeing to sell the penthouse to Irene and Tom Clarkson.

Chapter 42

Maya

"Do you think we'll survive the sale of the other eleven residences?" I look over at Julian. He's on his side in my bed, staring at me.

We'd made love after I called Tom and Irene to tell them the news. They didn't care that it was near midnight. They both cried during the call, and it brought tears to my own eyes.

I was grateful that the deal was done because professionally it's taken me to a new level, but more than that I was thrilled that I could be an integral part of their life journey. I helped them find their forever home, and they'll spend countless holidays there with their children and grandchildren, filling the space with memories for even more generations to come.

"We'll work out a contract for that tomorrow." He slides his hand over his stomach. "Do you know how proud I am of you?"

I crawl on top of him, pressing my bare breasts against his chest. "I know that you are. You gave me an opportunity no one else would have. I can't thank you enough for that."

"One of the things I admire most about you…" His voice trails as he stops to tuck a strand of my hair behind my ear. "I admire your drive to succeed. You don't let anything get in your way. You fight for yourself. You need that to rise to the top in this town."

"One of the things I admire most about
you…" I stop to kiss his lips. "You're so supportive.
You want to see me shine. I need that in my life. I
want to be more like that too."

He pulls me closer for another soft kiss. "You
want to see others shine, Maya. I've seen that for
myself. You didn't push the Clarksons to purchase
the penthouse for your own selfish reasons."

I cock a brow. "I wanted that sale."

"Yes." He chuckles. "I agree, but you saw
something in them that day we danced with them. I
saw it in your eyes. You pictured them there. You
saw the way the place fit them as much as they fit into
the place. I think you knew it was their home before
they did."

I move to sit, rubbing my bare pussy over the
sheet that covers his groin. "You see the best in me."

His gaze travels over my body. "How can I
not when you're sitting naked on top of me?"

I giggle. "You know what I mean, Julian. You
see what I don't see."

"I see a beautiful woman who is determined
and strong."

I inch my hands up my stomach toward my
breasts. "What else do you see?"

"My future.
That stops my hands in place near my heart. "I want
to be that."

"You will be." He traces his fingertips over
my thighs. "The smartest move I've ever made was
falling in love with you."

***

"You are finally going to let me move in with you?" Tilly almost jumps into my arms. "I have been waiting for this day for years. We can have movie marathons and talk all night. When mom and dad come to visit, we'll let them stay with us, right. I don't want Frannie to. She can stay in a hotel."

I smirk. "What's the deal with you and Frannie?"

"Nothing," she answers too quickly. "I love her. When can I move in?"

I watch as she scans the living room of my apartment. She's already planning on rearranging the furniture to fit her stuff in. I can almost see her plotting it out as we speak.
"You can move in the day I move out."

She tilts her head. "You're joking. You're not moving out."

"I'm moving in with Julian." I start toward the kitchen. "On the stove, the back burner on the left doesn't work, so don't bother with it. You have to set the dishwasher to a fast cycle or you'll be paying too much for water. The woman who lives next door has a dog. He loves to bark at night, but since you're a vet assistant, I'm thinking that won't bother you one bit."

"Maya, stop." Her hand on my shoulder stops me just as I reach the sink. "You're moving in with him? Is it that serious?"

"I love him," I whisper.

"Scream it then." She hugs me from behind. "Oh my god, Maya. Scream it to the world. You're in love. What could be better than that?"

I pivot to face her. "If you were in love too. That's what would make it better."

Her kind blue eyes glide over my face. "I'll find him one day, or he'll find me. You need to be happy for you. I sure as hell am."

"I am happy," I confess as I hug her back. "He's the one, Tilly. I'm telling you Julian is the one for me."

"I know he is. I can see it in your eyes."

Chapter 43

Julian

"Why did you want to meet me here?" Maya sits on the bench next to me. We're in Bryant Park. The sun is high. The sky is blue. Life is perfect.

"My sister is having a baby." I turn to look at her. "She's known since the night of the launch party."

"Julian." She hugs me tightly. "You're going to be an uncle."

I am. It's a concept I can't quite grasp. When Brynn told me earlier today that she was expecting a baby, she cried. I held her and whispered to her how happy I was for her and Smith. I'm thrilled. I can't wait to meet their little one.

"And a godfather," I add. "I'll love that child. I love that child already."

Maya smiles as she trails her finger over my brow. "You're going to have so much fun with that baby. I have a blast every time I go home and see Frannie and her kids."

"I've never seen Brynn so happy before." I tug Maya close to my side.

She kisses my cheek. "When I saw her last week I told you she looked like she was glowing. Now we know why."

"She'll be an amazing mom."

She squints against the sun as she watches a woman and man pass by us. "I think so too. I don't know her well but from what I've seen she's patient and compassionate."

I shield my eyes from the sun with my hand. "Do you see that fenced off building over there?"

She glances to her left and the brick building that overlooks the park.

"You bought it, didn't you?"

My mouth curves into an easy smile. "I couldn't pass it up. The location alone…"

"Made it completely irresistible to you," she finishes my sentence as my voice trails.

She rests her head on my shoulder as she looks at the building. "Is that the next Bishop Hotel?"

I kiss her forehead softly, tenderly. "My grandfather lived there when he was a kid. I've been waiting my entire adult life for it to be sold. You're looking at the next Bishop Hotel, but this one will be different."

"Different, how?"

"Smaller rooms, affordable rates." I take in a deep breath. "He would have wanted it that way. It's going to be ideal for families with children, college kids or anyone who wants to see this city without burning through their bank account."

"I like that idea." She smiles up at me. "Budget Bishop Hotel."

I huff out a laugh. "Not quite, but we'll work on the branding."

"I never met the man, but I think he'd be proud of his grandson today."

"I wonder about that sometimes. If he was still here, I wonder if he'd tell me I've done him proud. I think this new hotel will help me feel like I've done what I set out to do."

"You have a few years left to make your mark on the world, Julian." She smiles up at me. "You can do a lot of good in this city if you set your mind to it."

"We can do a lot of good." I brush my lips against her forehead. "Together we can do anything."

***

I lick a trail from her breasts down her stomach to the very top of her mound. I rest my lips there, kissing her softly while she catches her breath.

"I have a showing in thirty minutes." She looks at her wrist, but she's not wearing a watch. Not that it would do any good. I made a promise to her that I'd buy her a new watch on her birthday, but she scoffed at the idea. She wears vintage watches because it fits who she is.

Her eyes settle on the tattoo on her wrist.

"You're everything," I whisper the words that she hears every time I catch her looking at the tattoo. "You're my everything."

Her hand smooths my hair back from my forehead. "I'm enough. I know that I am."

She's my world. We came back here after we sat on the bench at Bryant Park. It's the middle of the day, but the need was strong. I didn't have to ask if she wanted to take my cock in her mouth once we got home.

She stripped, crawled on the bed and licked her lips. I gave it to her as she moaned. She took it all, fingering her pussy to orgasm before swallowing my release.

"That's not enough time for me to make you come." I lick the seam of her pussy tenderly. "I want to take my time with you."

She spreads her legs. "You can do it, Julian. You have fifteen minutes and then I need to be out the door."

"A challenge?" I look at her face. "How can I resist that?"

Her eyelids flutter shut. "You can't."

She's right about not being able to resist, but it's her, not the challenge that makes me want her to feel as much pleasure as she can.

"I love you, Julian," she moans as her hands fist in my hair.

My breath gusts over her hot flesh as I whisper the words back to her. "I love you. I'll never stop."

Epilogue

Six Months Later

Maya

I look down at the picture on Julian's phone. "Little Caroline Booth is a dream. How can a baby be that cute?"

"It's all her mother." He winks at me. "She looks exactly like Brynn and nothing like Smith."

He may be right. It's too early to tell who she looks like. "I think she's going to be a perfect combination of both of them."

"She's going to be the unofficial flower girl at their wedding next month." He closes his phone and shoves it back in his jacket pocket. "Brynn has a dress all picked out for the baby. It'll be a day to remember."

It will be. I've gotten closer to both Brynn and her fiancé Smith these past few months. We have dinner once a week with them, and when Brynn went into labor, Smith insisted that both Julian and I head to the hospital. We did. We were able to see Caroline soon after she was born and I was lucky enough to witness Julian's parents meeting their granddaughter for the very first time.

We've talked about having children since then, but we're happy with just the two of us for now.

It will be part of our future, one day when we know the time is right.

"You've sold more than half of the residences, Maya." Julian smiles at me before he sits on the edge of our bed. "Three more to go and our work together is done."

I'll miss it although I rarely see Julian in an official capacity at this point. He's been busy developing plans for the new hotel near Bryant Park, and I've had my hands full with selling the residences in the hotel in Chelsea as well as a few apartments.

I've also picked up a handful of new clients. Many of them I met when they wanted to view one of the units in the hotel. I've listed two apartments this week for sale. Both are charming condos on the Upper West Side.

My business is growing. Anne is thrilled, and I'm thankful that I can go to work every single day to a job I love. I'm also grateful that my sister and I are closer than we've ever been. Tilly took on a roommate to help cover rent. It's been a solid investment property for me, and she's turned it into a home.

"How's Charlie working out?" I unbutton my blouse. "I didn't see him when I dropped by your office yesterday."

He watches my hands. "Good. He's going to fit in just fine."

The day Isadora quit I could tell that Julian felt a load being taken off his shoulders. She decided to go work for a competitor. It might have been a move to push Julian's buttons, but it didn't work. He wished her well with me by his side and then he had his attorney negotiate the purchase of Isadora's shares in Bishop Hotels. It cost him a lot but he told me it was worth every dime. That was two months ago and since then, he hasn't heard a word.

"You're still dressed," I point out as I undo the clasp on the front of my bra. "I thought you promised me a shower before bed."

He hangs his head. "We need to talk, Maya."

I'm only wearing panties. He's still fully dressed. "I'll get my robe."

"No." He pats the bed. "Come sit here."

I move to sit next to him. "What is it?"

My heart pounds in my chest. I'm not scared. I know that whatever he says to me, it won't be words of regret or disappointment. We address every problem we have with frank discussion and honesty. We never go to bed upset with one another and we almost always fall asleep in each other's arms.

Our dinner together earlier was perfect. We'd gone to the Bishop Hotel penthouse to see Tom and Irene Clarkson. They'd cooked us dinner, as they've done once before. We laughed together and then danced to a Sinatra song as the sun set.

The only thing that has changed since then is that I've fallen more in love with Julian. I do every minute of every day.

"I love you, Julian."

He moves quickly then. It's a blur as he drops to one knee in front of me.

"Maya." His voice quakes in a way I've never heard before. "I had written this out. I had rehearsed every word and now I can't remember any of it."
He tugs a small box from the inner pocket of his suit jacket before he opens it to reveal a beautiful ring. It's

a pear-shaped sapphire stone surrounded by small diamonds. It's unique, and original. It's totally me.

"Marry me, Maya." He slides the ring from the box onto my finger. "I love you more than anything. I'd give my life for yours. You make me happier than any man deserves to be and if you marry me, I promise you right here and right now, that I will put you before me until I draw my last breath."

"I'll marry you," I whisper as I cup his face in my hands. "You know how deeply I love you. How much I adore everything about you."

"We'll make each other happy until our last days." He kisses me softly. "Whatever it takes to put a smile on this beautiful face, I'll do it."

"Love me forever, Julian. That's all it will take to put a smile on my face."

"I promise I will. I promise that every single day until my last on this earth, I will tell you how much I love you."

That's all I need. This man, this life and the future we will build together are more than I ever could have asked for.

Preview of HUSH
From the Just This Once Series

I have three hard and fast rules when it comes to one-night stands.

Don't tell her your last name.

Don't take her home with you.

Don't knock her up.

I'm screwed.

Jane Smith was supposed to be a quick fling. I saw her as a brief escape from the never-ending drama that is my life as a surgeon in New York City.

Now, she's pregnant and scared as hell.

Oh, and apparently her real name is *Chloe Newell.*

It's probably not the best time to tell her that I'm the guy who ruined her life two years ago.

Author's Note: *This romance contains a gorgeous doctor, an unexpected pregnancy and a past connection between the hero and heroine that could change everything. HUSH is part of the Just This Once Series. Each book features a different couple and the books are not connected so they can be read in any order.*

Chapter 1

Evan

"I'm not a coward. I am not a coward." A soft, smooth feminine voice catches me off guard.

I turn toward it and grab a quick glimpse of what looks like the world's most perfect ass in a pair of black lace panties. They vanish the second the woman in question stands upright again, the red umbrella in her hand mangled from the brutal wind.

"You don't strike me as a coward, sweetheart." I raise my near-empty glass of bourbon in a mock toast because any person brave enough to venture out in December in a New York City blizzard dressed like it's the middle of July deserves a medal. This one earns bonus points for having an ass that can halt a snowstorm in its path.

That may or may not be a fact, but the timing is sure as hell spot-on.

The deluge of snow that has blanketed the city for the past five hours has stopped abruptly. That wasn't the case up until a minute ago when I was standing, alone, outside this hotel contemplating what my next move will be.

Big picture stuff, not which-of-my-casual-hookups-should-I-call-tonight stuff.

"Thanks, stranger." She smooths her hands over the short skirt of her frilly navy blue dress as she takes in the length of my six foot plus frame. "I'm not your sweetheart, though."

Wheat blonde hair, hazel eyes, glossy full pink lips, and an attitude.

Forget the big picture. My next move needs to involve this woman.

My eyes don't leave her angelic face even though I want to trail my gaze and my mouth over every inch of her body. "Fair enough. Introduce yourself, and while you're at it, I'd love to meet your imaginary friend too."

I can't resist the urge to look when her nipples furl into hard points beneath the airy fabric of her dress. As much as I want that reaction to be from the rich baritone of my voice, I suspect it's from the burst of wind that just picked up her skirt. There's a brief flash of sheer lace covering smooth skin before she yanks the hem of the skirt back in place.

My evening just got a whole hell-of-a-lot better.

"My imaginary friend?" She tucks a piece of her windswept hair behind her ear. My fist clenches in envy. I want those waves balled in my hand so tightly that the only noise she makes is one that tells me she wants my cock deeper.

I crack a smile. "You were hell bent on convincing someone that you're not a coward. Since we're the only two out here and there's no phone in your hand, I take it that your imaginary friend is the asshole who thinks you're a coward. I'll argue your case if you point me in his direction, or is it her direction?"

"Are you a lawyer?"

I'll be anything she wants me to be. I'm a surgeon, vascular to be precise, and I have to be.

Tonight, I don't want to be Dr. Evan Scott. I'd rather be the star of her future fantasies; that one awe-inspiring lay all women look back on for the rest of their life when they get themselves off.

"Not guilty." I hold my hand up in mock surrender. "Your name, beautiful. What is it?"

Her thickly lashed eyes widen as the heavy metal awning above us creaks under the weight of the wet snow. "It's Jane. Jane Smith."

She's the third *Jane Smith* I've met this month.

I'm not offended that the name offered is as fake as the smile plastered on the face of the doorman who is watching our every move from the warm comfort of the lobby. Experience has taught me that women in this town hide behind a false persona for just three reasons.

One is that their wedding ring is tucked in a pocket or a purse and they don't want the night to seep into their two kids, bake sales, walking the dog in the park, day-to-day life.

For the record, I avoid those women at all costs. They're easy to spot, even if they think they're fooling everyone, including themselves.

The second reason women morph into Jane Smith, Jane Doe or just plain Jane is they're prepping to hand over a fake number.

Eye contact is everything, and if a woman I'm after can't make it with me, I tap out. There are too many women on this island who are interested in what I'm offering. I'm not into wasting my time on someone whose type isn't tall with dark brown hair, blue eyes, muscular pecs, that cut V that women dream of, and a thick nine-inch cock.

Yeah, I measured. Every man does. He's a fucking liar if he doesn't admit it.

The third reason is why my new blonde friend tossed out the name Jane Smith to me just now. She's looking for the same thing I am. One night of no-personal-details, uninhibited, I-dare-you-to-walk-straight-after-that fucking.

"It's nice to meet you, Jane." I extend a hand because in public I'm always the perfect gentleman.

She takes a step forward, dragging her sorry looking umbrella behind her. Her hand lands in mine for a soft shake. It's just enough pressure to stir my cock. "What's your name, stranger?"

I could easily be the Jack to her Jane, but I want to hear my name from those lips tonight. "Evan."

The look on her face is all surprise and awe like I've already got two fingers inside her and I'm honed in on that spot that will etch my name into her memory forever. "Is that your real name?"

I crane my neck to look at the lobby. The last thing I need right now is for anyone I work with to breeze past us and call me *Dr. Scott.* I have to get this woman into a hotel room and out of that dress now.

"According to my driver's license, it is." I circle the pad of my thumb on her palm before I let her hand go. "I'm going inside to refill my drink and then I'm heading upstairs. Can I get you anything, Jane?"

She reaches up to touch her neck. It's a subtle sign that she wants my hand, or maybe my mouth, there. "Are you inviting me up to your room?"

Technically, I'm inviting her to a room I haven't rented yet. I was out here catching a breath of frigid nor'easter air. I did my time inside when I took the podium, ran through an off-the-cuff speech about the boatload of accolades my boss acquired in his career and then handed him a silver wristwatch courtesy of his wife. He threw the goddamn shindig on his own dime and then expected me to kiss ass in public to hold onto a job I'm not sure I want.

"If you are, I'm game," Jane tosses that jewel out before I have a chance to offer a formal invitation to get naked with me. "I didn't notice you at the ceremony. Are you a friend of the bride or the groom?"

It's the obvious conclusion to jump to. I'm dressed in a tuxedo. There's a wedding reception in the ballroom tonight. She has no clue that I was just in the hotel's five-star restaurant with a group that consists of primarily sixty-something-year-old surgeons all desperate to one-up each other with elaborate descriptions of their summer homes.

At thirty-four I'm the baby of the bunch, hence the reason I'm standing in the bitter cold with a drink in my hand contemplating why I went to medical school in the first place.

Jane marches on, nerves twitching at the edge of her words. "I'm a friend of Leanna. I'm actually one of her bridesmaids. I had to get the hell out of there when Henry started talking about how committed he is to her. It's bullshit. You know that, don't you? He totally screwed her over this past summer when he was in Vegas. She forgave him and now they're married. Can you believe that?"

"Henry is a selfish son-of-a-bitch."

Her eyes flick up to meet mine. "What's your room number?"

The snow starts again, large flakes of unwanted inconvenience. I need a condom. My gaze darts up and down the street. Other than a restaurant a block over, every other storefront and business are locked up tight.

Late Sunday night will do that to Manhattan. A snowstorm doesn't help.

"You have protection, right?" Pretty Jane reads my mind like a sensual sorceress. "I didn't bring any condoms with me."

Normally, I'd have at least a few tucked in my pocket, but I got dressed at the hospital. An emergency surgery this afternoon cut into my prep time for this hellish evening, so I had my rental tux delivered. I changed in the locker room and forgot one of the essentials. The breath mints made it into my pants pocket next to my wallet, but the condoms didn't.

Fucking great.

I'm not sending this woman on a mission to get me a rubber. That comes with the risk of her bailing on me because she doesn't see the effort as worth the reward.

It's worth it, in spades, or in her case, orgasms.

"I've got that covered, or should I say, it will be covered," I quip with a tip of my glass before I down the last swallow. I'll go floor-by-floor and door-to-door in this hotel to find a condom if need be. "Do you need to say goodbye to Leanna before you bail?"

She blows an adorable puff of air out from between her lips. "I do. I left my purse in there. What about you?"

"I didn't have a purse that matched my outfit tonight," I joke. "I'll meet you in the lobby in thirty minutes. We can head up to the room together."

"Make it fifteen," she counters, a challenge woven into her tone. "I'll take a London Fog."

"Consider it done," I whisper as she breezes past me, the maimed umbrella dragging behind her. The doorman jumps into action and props open the heavy glass door. Jane steps into the vestibule just as the ugly winter wind gives not only me but the doorman, the early holiday gift of an eyeful of her luscious ass.

Something tells me this night is going to be one for the record books.

Coming soon

Preview of BARE
From the Just This Once Series

The first and last one-night stand I had ended with zero orgasms for me and my wallet gone.

I fell asleep after the man who called himself *Kent* rolled off of me and out of my life.

The only thing he left behind was a business card on the floor next to the bed.

Griffin Kent. Attorney at Law.

Since I don't know a soul in New York, I head straight to the jerk's office on Madison Avenue to get back my wallet and reclaim my pride.

I'm not prepared for what happens when I arrive at the prestigious law firm of Kent & Colt.

I doubt that the real Griffin Kent would leave a woman unsatisfied in any way. He's tall, dark haired and dangerously handsome. He's also the complete opposite of the imposter I spent the night with.

The arrogant attorney orders his assistant to help me, but he's the one who enrolls in the art class I came to Manhattan to teach.

He may be my student, but something tells me that Griffin is going to be schooling me in the art of seduction.

Author's Note: *This sexy standalone novel contains a dirty talking attorney, nude male models and a HEA the hero will do anything to fight for. BARE is part of the Just This Once Series. Each book features a different couple and since the books are not connected, they can be read in any order.*

Chapter 1

Piper

"Griffin Kent is the worst lover I've ever had."
With tears welling in the corners of my eyes, I stare at
the woman sitting behind the sleek wooden reception
desk. "I can't believe I slept with him. I called the
police. They're going to be here any minute."

She looks past me to the frosted glass doors at
the entrance of the law offices of Kent & Colt. "If it's
a crime to be a dud in bed, my ex-husband would be
serving twenty to life right now."

I scrub my hand over my face, mascara
staining my palm. "I didn't call them because of that."

"Can I get you a glass of water?" The kind-
looking woman is on her feet now. "You look about
ready to pass out. Why don't you sit down? We can
discuss this."

Discuss what? I went to a hotel with a man
last night, we had really bad sex and when I woke up
an hour ago, he was gone along with my wallet and
my smartphone.

"I don't want to talk about it." I look beyond
her to the massive, exquisitely designed space that
obviously houses a number of offices. "Where's the
asshole? I need to see him now."

Her lips curl into an unexpected smile. "He's
not here. He never gets in until at least nine fifteen."

My gaze drops to my wrist but the silver watch I always wear isn't there. "He took everything from me."

The middle-aged woman rounds the reception desk until she's next to me, her arm slung over my shoulder. "You listen to me. I don't know what happened between you and Mr. Kent, but there's not a man on the face of this earth who can take everything from a woman."

Great.

I'm in the middle of a crisis and this woman is on her soapbox preaching about the merit of my inner strength.

Griffin Kent took that from me too.

"I don't know what to do," I mutter to myself.

The self-appointed cheerleader next to me adds her two cents even though I didn't ask for it. "You're going to calm down and let me help you. What's your name, dear?"

I feel like I should covet every ounce of personal information after what just happened to me. I was open and trusting when I met the attractive man in the bar last night. I told him my name when he asked. He reciprocated by telling me his. Kent.

An hour later we were in a hotel room and I was proud of myself for checking a one-night stand off my bucket list. I need to wipe that list clean now and focus on one thing and one thing only.

Find some common sense and use it.

"Where are the police? I used the phone at the front desk to call them before I left the hotel. They should be here by now." I stare down at my dress. It's silver shimmer, low cut and much too short to see the light of day. I'd never wear this in broad daylight and yet, here I am.

Thank the heavens above that my parents are in Denver, completely oblivious to what their only child is doing on her third day in New York City. The move here was supposed to change my life, not drive the entire thing into a ditch at high speed.

"I think we can straighten this out without involving the NYPD."

"How?" I face the woman. She reminds me of my first art teacher in high school. That shouldn't offer me any comfort, but it does. "He needs to be arrested and thrown in jail after what he did to me."

"Were you hurt?" Her eyes scan my face, locking on my green eyes.

I know exactly what I look like. I didn't have time to shower when I crawled out of the hotel room bed, but I did catch a glimpse of myself in the bathroom mirror. My makeup was beyond repair. My shoulder length brown hair was such a mess that I used a bright pink hair elastic to tie it up into a tight ponytail.

At least, Griffin Kent left behind my clutch with the hair elastic, a tube of lipstick and my apartment keys inside of it.

Either the bastard has a heart, or he overlooked my keys as he was stealing my wallet.

"He didn't hurt me." I fiddle with the business card in my hand. "He took my wallet and my phone when I fell asleep. My watch too. He took it all."

"I find it very hard to believe that Mr. Kent is responsible for this."

Of course she'd say that. She's the first face anyone sees when they come through the doors of this law office. It's on Madison Avenue. I doubt like hell that her monthly paycheck has less than five zeroes at the end of it. I'd say that's well above the going rate for what blind faith costs in this city.

I shove the business card at her. "I have the proof right here."

She reaches to take the now tattered card from me, but I hold tight to the corner of it. It's evidence. He left this behind. I found it on the carpeted floor of the hotel room next to one of my heeled sandals that I'd kicked off before I got into bed with the thieving bastard.

Griffin Kent. Attorney at Law. It's right there in black raised lettering on the card.

If that's not proof, I don't know what is.

"Did he give that to you?"

"He dropped it," I explain. "It must have fallen out of his pocket."

Her tongue skims over her front teeth. "What does Mr. Kent look like?"

I survey the office. There's no movement anywhere. I can hear muffled voices in the distance, but I haven't seen another soul since I walked through the doors to the reception area.

Since the hotel I was at is on Columbus and Eighty-first, I walked here though Central Park. I spent the bulk of that time rehearsing what I was going to say to Kent once I saw him. I never expected to be subjected to a pre-confrontation interview by his receptionist.

"You know what he looks like," I bite back with a sigh. "I know that he spent the night with me and then robbed me blind."

"Humor me, dear." She gives my shoulder a squeeze. "Describe Mr. Kent to me."

If it's going to take that to chase away the look of doubt that's plastered all over her expression, I'll give her what she wants. "He's the same height as me, blonde hair, full beard, really nice brown eyes."

"What the hell is going on here?" The low rumble of a deeply seductive voice asks from behind me.

"Mr. Kent." The woman next to me turns quickly. "This young woman is here looking for … well, sir, I think I'll let her explain why she's here."

Mr. Kent? The voice I just heard isn't the same one that invited me up to that hotel room last night. I turn around.

Dark brown hair, blue eyes, a smooth chiseled jaw and a face so handsome that women must stop and stare when he passes them by. I know I would. I can't tear my gaze from him now.

"I'm Griffin Kent," he says smoothly as he nears me. "And you are?"

Coming Soon

THANK YOU

Thank you for purchasing my book. I can't even begin to put to words what it means to me. If you enjoyed it, please remember to write a review for it. Let me know your thoughts! I want to keep my readers happy.

For more information on new series and standalones, please visit my website, www.deborahbladon.com. There are book trailers and other goodies to check out.

If you want to chat with me personally, please LIKE my page on Facebook. I love connecting with all of my readers because without you, none of this would be possible.
www.facebook.com/authordeborahbladon

Thank you, for everything.

ABOUT THE AUTHOR

Deborah Bladon has never read a romance hero she didn't like. Her love for romance novels began when she was old enough to board the bus, library card in hand to check out the newest Harlequin paperbacks. She's a Canadian by heart, and by passport, but you can often spot her in New York City sipping a latte and looking for inspiration for her next story. Manhattan is definitely her second home.

She cherishes her family and believes that each day is a gift for writing, for reading, and for loving.

Printed in Great Britain
by Amazon